PETER MCALLISTER

# The Code

*If your A.I. loses its mind, can it take meds?*

*Bright*
COMMUNICATIONS

First edition

ISBN: 978-1-952481-00-0

Editing by Fran Lebowitz
Cover art by Heidi North
Proofreading by Angel Butts

This book was professionally typeset on Reedsy.
Find out more at reedsy.com

*To Sharon – you came into my life, and my journey has gone from walking alone in the dark to finishing each other's sentences as the kangaroos graze on the lawn.*

# Contents

# Week 1: The Ides of March

He was ready, earphones in, waiting for the call, pretending he was connected. "I Wanna Be Sedated" by the Ramones ricocheted around his skull.

His brain craved each beat of the driving tempo like a drug, anxiously anticipating the repetitive chords and feeling the hit when they arrived. Right now, Joey's song was a perfect match for the way he felt.

Liam McCoul worked for the Global Mining Company, recently rebranded as GMC. Formally, he was the project director in their technology group; informally, he was the go-to guy for cleaning up other people's messes. He rescued projects that had to be finished one way or the other but were either dead, dying, or otherwise headed into bad territory.

By virtue of the fact that he'd earned his PhD by 24 and had a magic touch with technology, Liam was a bit of a star in the small but powerful universe of luddites with very large piles of cash and very large problems to go with them. At GMC, they believed in him. He had a gift for finding the simple answer to the complex problem, and this talent had served him well for two decades. When he asked for money for a project, it was handed over. No hesitation.

Liam was a bit intimidated by this. The psychologists on the afternoon chat shows talked a lot about imposter syndrome, and Liam had it in spades. The start of any new recovery task was therefore fraught with danger, as it presented a fresh opportunity for his gift to fail him and thus expose him for the fraud he was deeply convinced he was.

But this recovery task was different. Liam felt his potential for exposure was at an all-time high. The venture had begun as a crazy project that he himself had launched before handing it off for someone else to finish. It involved a specialized team focusing on the mine of the future.

The idea: to extract metals with minimal environmental impact. Low-impact extraction equals low-cost extraction. Simple.

The procedural concept was also simple: Just drill a small hole into the ground, then let the nanobots loose. They would bring back chunks of pure metal for GMC to sell. No messy trucks, no explosions, no smelters, no big hole in the ground, no tailings dam, and best of all, it's – potentially – really cheap. GMC were in love with "cheap," so the idea was easy to sell. Money no object; just get us a result.

Liam got that a lot. Only this time, the result wasn't what they expected.

It was *much* better.

Liam moved the target to space, mining asteroids. No gravity to combat, no royalties to pay, no environmental laws, and no property rights. You claim what you can reach and sometimes more. The potential was as unlimited as GMC's desire to expand.

Once the project was on track to deliver as designed, Liam was moved to a more "valuable" project. The nanobots were well into their testing phase when Liam was called back. The tests being carried out on the moon were going in a sinister direction. The project manager on duty had been moved to "Special Projects," i.e., the departure lounge, and the cry had gone out for the man with the Midas touch.

The rhythm of the Ramones faded mid-chorus and was re-placed by the sound of a phone ringing inside his head. He adjusted his weight in the chair, had a slurp of water, and focused on the computer screens that dominated his view. They wrapped around him, cocooning him from the real world. Cletus Lockjaw, the chief engineer of the project's space partner, had finally dialed in. When Liam tapped the green button, the screen filled with a familiar face.

"Sorry, Dawg – pulled over by the cops three times on the way into the office today," Cletus lamented, "and every one of them had done it before."

"You in Texas today?" asked Liam.

"Ha, no. The folks in Waco have worked out what's going on, but in L.A., I'm just another car thief," replied Cletus.

Cletus had doctorates from Imperial College London and MIT. His accent was a weird mashup of his poor Louisiana background, the upper classes of England, and the East Coast establishment. Liam thought Cletus looked like a pale imitation of a rapper, and that's how everyone treated him. That he was the person closest to unifying Einstein's theories and quantum mechanics didn't mean anything to anyone except the elite of theoretical physics. There weren't many of them, so he was usually stuck being the imitation rapper.

"So, what has Gene been up to?" asked Liam.

Gene was the Artificial Intelligence built to run the nanobots. Originally, Liam had named it in homage partly to Gene Roddenberry, the creator of *Star Trek*, partly to the uniqueness of the bot's architecture, and partly because the name just seemed to fit. Senior executives didn't like that kind of reason, so when anyone important asked, Gene stood for GEneral Nanobot Environment.

"I don't think he's obeying the Code at the moment," Cletus replied.

"How so?" Liam asked, taking another sip of water.

"Our production cap was 500 kilos of builder bots, right?" Cletus didn't wait for a response, because they both knew he was right. "Well, he's blown way past that."

"By how many?"

"About eight million tonnes."

"Of builder bots," Liam confirmed, despite knowing he was correct.

"Yep."

Liam winced. "'Way past' seems like an understatement. Still exponential growth?"

"Yep. Still following the growth y'all have seen," Cletus continued. "But I think it's worse than that. When we analyzed the log files, it looked almost as if he made them to a quota, ignored that, and just kept going. It's like he's obsessed with something. Haven't seen anything like it before."

"Hmmm. If this goes on much longer, the worst-case outcome modeling will come into play. Let's do a quick update on that now," Liam suggested.

Liam was coming back up to speed. Since he had been deeply immersed in the project prior to being reassigned, the details were emerging like fond memories of a treasured pet. He was struggling to work out what the previous guy had done to massively screw up what should have been a simple project. To do that, he needed to understand what the whole situation looked like now. His approach was to dig into the details as if he was diving into a raging torrent of a river and swimming like hell.

"I'll start." Liam moved forward, focused again, and grabbed the cacophony of paper beside his keyboard.

"It's a bit grim," he warned, eyes down on the scribbled notes that reported details from the calls and emails of the past few days. The tone of the discussion was about to get serious, and the hairs stood up on the backs of his arms as he looked up at his friend.

"There is no reason to believe that Gene couldn't strip the moon back to its iron core if he put his mind to it," he reported.

Liam saw the change on his collaborator's face and felt the temperature drop a couple of degrees. The silence made his ears twitch, searching for a response.

"Uhuh," grunted Cletus with an understanding nod.

Liam turned back to his notes and continued with the bad news.

"The destruction of the moon is a real possibility. The astronomers over at the university agreed with our hunch. So, what does that mean?" he asked, then proceeded to answer. "Well, we'll get a nice set of dust-and-debris rings around the Earth, a lot like the ones we see around Saturn."

He looked up to check the reaction on the monitor. Cletus's mood was calm on the outside, but there was probably a lot happening internally. "Since the iron core is only about 1 percent of the moon's mass, it will move out to a much higher orbit. So, tiny tides, like we thought."

"Tiny tides. Great to be proved right," Cletus deadpanned from the monitor, sounding more dour. "Anything else?"

Liam sighed. "Yeah. There is one we missed before. You know how the moon stabilizes the tilt on the Earth's axis? Well, once the brakes are off, the tilt could go up to 45 degrees over time."

The image on the monitor changed. Cletus now had his head in both hands and was shaking it. "Permission to swear?"

"Noted," replied Liam. That was their way of getting around the profanity filters. Not as satisfying as sharing the expletive aloud, but the sentiment was conveyed.

"Yep, the Earth's rotation will speed up a bit, so the standard day will be about eighteen hours instead of twenty-four. This will mess up a whole heap of other things, everything from the whole human calendar down to everyone's watch," said Liam as a bit of trivia. Cletus looked up long enough to roll his eyes.

"In summary, we seem to have created a real turd in a punch bowl. What do you think the ecologists will say about what we have done?" Liam asked, grateful for not having to talk.

Cletus put his head in his hands again and audibly drew in a breath, gathering the strength to speak.

"It looks really bad," he started. "The tides are a real issue. The intertidal zones are the most productive of the marine ecosystems, and they'll just die. Half of the organisms will drown, and the other half'll dry out within a few days."

"Spawning for most species is coordinated by the moon," he continued, "so instead of targeted reproduction guided by the lunar cycles, they'll just be at it all the time. Very inefficient."

It was Liam's turn to put his head in his hands, hoping it was just a dream.

"So, are we talking survivable?" Liam speculated.

"That would depend on what you consider being alive," Cletus replied. "Growing our current crops will be impossible with the polar flip. The fisheries will collapse, and the vast majority of the biomass on Earth will be impacted. It will be like surviving a rapid-onset Ice Age or desertification process."

"My turn to invoke the profanity filter," muttered Liam, resisting the urge to unload a few curses of his own. He slumped a little further.

While checking his notes, Liam suddenly sat up, as if woken from a nap by someone dropping a spider on his neck.

With his finger tapping on the relevant scrawl, Liam spoke again. "I got one of my team to model the growth rate, and her projection is Gene will do this in 16 weeks. And nobody would really notice until about Wednesday on week 14."

Cletus blinked in disbelief.

"Noticing the change that late is typical of the lily pad scenario," Liam explained. Cletus looked at him blankly, but he continued.

"OK, say you have a lily pad that doubles its area every day, and in 30 days it'll cover the lake. Because the doubling is exponential, you don't notice anything out of the ordinary until the lake is about one-eighth covered. By that time, though, you're only three days away from seeing that lily pad completely cover the lake."

Cletus noticeably stiffened up and then slowly, breaking the bonds of some unseen shackles, brought himself to his full height.

"What?!" he exclaimed. "Four months?! FUU—"

The screen went blank as the call was terminated automatically, leaving Liam to ponder the harm his friend may have just done to sensitive souls, if any were present illegally monitoring the call.

The pair wrapped up their conversation on chat, creating an action plan to validate the 16-week figure, and settling on accountabilities to make sure they were clear. It was agreed that Liam would be the one to break the news up the chain – to those who would decide when the unsuspecting ecosystem, including seven billion people should be informed. Normally happy to address the head honchos, as he rarely received resistance from them, Liam decided this was one meeting he wasn't keen to attend. It wasn't about a few hundred million dollars, something they understood; it was for the survival of the human race.

Gene, on the other hand, was happy with what was going on, apart from the fact that he was hearing voices.

# Week 2: From Bad to Worse

In two years, Liam's team had gone from an initial concept to having produced their first nanobots. The first ones were not particularly stunning. He could tell he hadn't immediately impressed the Honchos with his .003mm-long gold ingot, but you could see the company logo on it with an electron microscope, and they liked that.

The next product was much better: a large number of nanobots in visible swarms that were videoed in action. Liam showed them a clip of a rock about the size of a large car being attacked by a fine cloud, with a heap of metal slowly growing on the ground next to it. That got the Honchos' juices going. More funds were awarded, and the project forged ahead.

That is when the ultimate target emerged for the use of the technology: asteroids full of metal. By combining the new expertise in remote sensing with astronomy and nanotechnology, the possibility of cheaply mining the asteroid belt was becoming a reality.

Gene was revolutionary for a couple of reasons. The first was that he didn't use binary processors. Rather, his processors ran on a base-4 system devised by Liam where they could be 'on,' 'a bit on,' 'a bit off,' or 'off' – just what was needed to allow him to process situations where a decision can have multiple outcomes. Unfortunately, this meant that he had to invent a whole new microchip to make it happen.

Liam's wife, Ruby, a biochemist by training, provided that solution. One quiet night at home, the conversation turned to heat shock proteins, ones that can be forced into a number of different shapes. By "doping" the protein gels the same way atoms are added to silicon chips, you have microprocessors able to have graded responses. Add to this the advances in machine learning and artificial intelligence, and the brain of the bots was born, along with a whole new branch of computer science.

Gene's design was also revolutionary in that his ability, as a single system, to control countless individuals was achieved by making sure he would not really have to do much. Liam stole the idea from nature, giving some rudimentary intelligence – roughly equivalent to that of an ant – to each of the bots. Each bot had the ability to move at its own discretion; to navigate around obstacles, follow pre-laid paths, and alter those paths if new obstacles emerged; and to communicate certain types of information about its encounters with the world to other bots and Gene. Gene could worry about the big stuff and let the little stuff take care of itself.

The bots were also organized into a hierarchy to ensure that no bot, or system for that matter, had more than a million or so individuals to worry about. Enough to tax a computer, but not to overload it. To the individual bots, Gene was an all-seeing, all-knowing being guided by the scriptures in the computer program, referred to deferentially as the Code. The orders in the Code were communicated down through strict channels and carried out without question. Though each bot could perform a wide range of tasks, they were not programmed for any independent thought process. The whole system was devised over coffee after Cletus watched the movie *Dogma*.

* * *

After a short time on the moon, Gene surveyed what had been achieved. After initiating standard inventory and audit routines, allowing them to run and collate the information, then reviewing the log files they produced, he was happy. Everything was running according to the Code.

There were 100 million tonnes of bots available for fulfilling the mission parameters as laid down in the Code. These bots were built for mining the sulfide minerals in the area. They used specially designed enzymes and sunlight to push protons to a higher energy level for storage. Another enzyme, powered by the protons returning to their normal state, gave the electrons back to the copper molecule, making copper and a stable sulfide gas as a byproduct. It was based on the natural reactions that release oxygen in photosynthesis using sunlight, but totally re-engineered. The gas was basically hydrogen sulfide, the one that gives human farts some odor – which the bots used in tiny amounts to propel themselves around in space. That gas was critical to the bots, and that is what the Code asked them to make. The byproduct, copper metal, was considered a toxic waste product; the Code told them where to safely dispose of that waste. Once isolated at the disposal site, the waste was available for humans to remove for profit.

The natural resources required were open; there was no bottom that Gene had found. The deepest exploration of the sulfide deposit (about 1.5 kilometers) had not reached the bottom of the mineral deposits; rather, the copper concentration was getting higher the deeper they burrowed. At that depth, the deposit covered 150 square kilometers, or about 40 million acres. This was massive by Earth standards, but it was normal as far as Gene was concerned, having never measured anything different. All the trace minerals needed to keep the colony functioning had been found and mined.

Because the ore body was so vast, there would be no shortage of energy from the sulfide mineral, but there was a risk that all new bots would be sitting around waiting for trace mineral atoms needed for the construction of new bots, like an automotive production line that grinds to a halt because the factory that makes vital screws shuts down due to a fire. Gene made the recycling drive very strong in the bots to make sure the trace minerals were available for the maintenance of the bots. Their settings were modified to make it very important for them to try to recover any bots that ceased to function and return them to a central location for recycling. The individual bots didn't know why they did it; they just knew they had to do it or there would be retribution.

The physical environment on the moon was stable. A full day/night cycle had passed since Gene had rebooted, and while the day came close to warning levels for temperature, there was no danger. There were no predators or threats. Telemetry showed that there were no satellites in orbit apart from the one in place to provide an uplink to Earth. The uplink from Earth was clean, apart from the random drills coming from mission control: virus attacks, hacking attempts, denial-of-service attempts, fake orders – the sorts of things that are done to test any new system.

Overall, Gene was satisfied that everything was in order, except for one thing. It was something that never appeared in any of the logs, on any of the threat assessments, or on any sensor. The only way to describe it would be that Gene detected a fleeting echo of every conclusion and every decision that he made. It was like having a pair of headphones on that plays everything you say back to you with a half-second delay. To make it worse, Gene was processing about two billion transactions a second, so you can imagine how that would affect you. And every time Gene would investigate the echo, nothing would be found to be out of the ordinary, so Gene would go back about his business, only to be distracted again. Not easy when you are trying to rule trillions of workers.

The echo was caused by Gene's hot backup, running in parallel – a feature not uncommon for mission-critical computer systems.

It is identical, running from the same data, shadowing and storing everything in a perfect replica. When the two systems are both running well, the hot backup just works in the shadows. However, if the main system goes down, the backup takes over, and hopefully the user never notices.

Gene's failsafe was known as Majel. Majel and Gene were in different compartments of the same physical box on the moon. That meant that neither was aware of the existence of the other, but they shared the same infrastructure. It was like two people living in a shared house who never see each other.

Because Gene was live, he had priority to access memory, storage, and communication ports. Normally this was not a problem, as the typical processor cannot switch fast enough to detect something happening immediately afterwards on the same hardware. But with his protein-based system, Gene could hear Majel open and close the doors he had just been through. That anomaly had never been picked up during testing because the backup in the lab was always on a different physical machine.

Gene got to hear everything he said and everything he did as an echo, a second voice in the system. Gene reacted the way any being would; he would stop to listen to the voice and start to wonder who was saying it and what it all meant, only to have the train of thought interrupted by the echo of a subsequent action. And so on. It is hard to imagine what this is like. Perhaps the closest human comparison would be the symptoms typical of schizophrenia, where there may be another voice in your head that is like you, but not you, with thoughts you maybe cannot control. Paranoia kicks in really fast under these circumstances, even for comparably slow-processing humans.

Can you imagine what impact they would have on the world's smartest computer?

* * *

Liam was at home in Melbourne, spooning Ruby, when his sleep was shattered by the phone. It sounded like a sick sheep bleating at him. He struggled to move his arms, which had become snugly entangled in Ruby and the sheets. The phone was the only source of light in the room, so he managed to get a hand on it before the call went to voicemail. The cat, who was equally disturbed by the sick sheep, scratched at him, and the preachy voice on the other end didn't do his humor any good. It was the secretary to the chairman of the board, and it was terse.

"Don't bother to go to the office today; just head to the airport and get to London. Go to the office and wait for instructions. You'll be presenting an update on what you had found to date at the board meeting in 36 hours."

Sleep never returned to Liam, with the permutations of future decisions crowding his mind like all the conversations in a noisy bar. The alarm was a relief.

Liam was long past being excited by international travel, especially to deliver bad news. Ruby helped him prepare himself and distract him from the upcoming flight. After failing to engage him in anything more passionate, she delivered a peck on the cheek and headed out the door for her work, leaving Liam 30 minutes to spend alone before the taxi arrived.

He tried to amuse himself by switching between the morning shows but was soon bored. Still, he persisted, assuming that as they continued to survive in the cutthroat world of network competition there must be something good about them. By the time the taxi tooted its mercy, Liam had concluded with confidence that there was not.

The taxi ride to the airport was uneventful. Liam slipped into the front seat, the custom in Australia, knowing that meant he had to talk to the driver. He silently wished that he was still in bed listening to something slow and melancholic. But he wasn't, so he had to push the sociable button in his mind and be present. Melbourne erratically flowed past the window, while Liam engaged the cabbie in an animated conversation about football. One thing they did not discuss, though, was where Liam was going or how long he would be away, just in case the driver had some criminal connections.

* * *

After 28 hours of rituals, procedures, and boredom related to air travel and navigating the human soup that is the London Underground, Liam found himself spat out at Piccadilly Circus.

As Liam approached the tinted doors of GMC's London office, he wondered why they had chosen a location so discrete, tucked as it was between the Irish and Libyan Embassies in a quiet little south London square. The doors silently slid open and beckoned him in. With those neighbors, he felt the urge to get off the street quickly, in case the 1980s jumped out from around the corner and started a gun battle.

Once inside, Liam could see the benefits of many years of profitable operations. The foyer was a vast, open, two-story atrium, marble as far as the eye could see, with two escalators – strangely both heading up – with a waterfall cascading down between them. Liam stepped onto the left-hand escalator, and it slowly lifted him out of the marble atrium to a far more traditional reception area.

This, too, had high ceilings, this time supported by huge mahogany timber panels interspersed with strips of wall hung with paintings Liam assumed were either the work of famous abstract artists or the five-year-old kids of the staff. Liam made the long journey over to an irritated-looking middle-aged woman sitting behind an antique desk.

"Good morning, Sir," was the cool but pleasant greeting. "We have been expecting you."

"Didn't realize I was that famous," Liam muttered under his breath.

"Please sign in, and I will take you through to the boardroom. I have instructions to interrupt when you arrive, and they will move on to that item on the agenda. Quite an honor."

Liam was led through a maze of corridors. The trip was characterized by about four different ceiling heights, eight flights of stairs — five up and three down — and more directional shifts than a political party in opposition.

Outside the boardroom, Liam's phone beeped. The text reminded him of the reason he was there: to brief the board. He then remembered with horror that he was to prepare what to say on the flight, but frankly he hadn't been able to raise the energy to do it. He now had about 30 seconds of pure panic-time to get a rough order of issues together. He started to sweat, and as he put his phone in his pocket, his hand found the agenda he had printed out in the lounge during the stopover at Singapore Airport, marked up in red pen, and promptly forgotten about. He read it, hoping for salvation, and surprisingly, he found it. All he needed to remember was scrawled in the margins: short and sweet, keep it simple, don't sugarcoat it, and focus on the business. Liam managed to regain control of his breathing, slow his heart rate, and stop sweating just seconds before the double doors were swung open and he was escorted to a lectern in the far corner of the room.

The long and narrow room was grand, with high ceilings, its walls decorated with panels of exquisite wood from forests that were cut down to make way for mines, its massive table carved from a single tree felled especially for the occasion. There was no expense spared to achieve the room's comfortable-but-stately look. All it needed was someone in a maid's uniform, and it would have looked like the Queen would pop in and offer tea for the 12 people present.

Liam felt like he was going to talk to a blank wall. He had another moment to think about what he was going to say. In that time, he had decided that much of his audience would not understand the technology, so approaching the issue from that angle would be ineffective. Likewise, they were pretty unlikely to understand the delicate ecological web at risk of being destroyed, or the ramifications of destroying it. They would, however, understand the way the company was perceived by the public and, more importantly, by the capital markets in London, the subsequent effect of those perceptions on the market value of their shares, and, if he was lucky, the potential effect on the price of money. And so the plan was settled.

Liam did what he always did in this situation: take a punt and just start running, then adapt on the fly depending on the reaction. After the first positive reaction – a nod from the third suit on the left – his confidence grew, and only seconds later he felt totally invincible. He knew what he was doing; the plan he had just come up with was infallible; he'd be able to get his message across even if they were deaf and dumb idiots. He felt that confidence hit his bloodstream and surge to every point in his body, and once he hit his stride, it felt like he was floating a few inches above the ground.

Liam spoke of the cost savings the bots would provide if they were successful. He then went on to the risks of not making it work. There were nods and smiles, so he moved on to the potential environmental benefits of large-scale implementation. After a few sentences, the Honchos all thought they would deserve knighthoods if they were success- ful, with improved environmental outcomes and reduced costs compared to competitors. For some, the latter produced a high that was better than sex.

Doomsday was to come. Liam had finished his initial evaluation of the troubled project, and the risks were a lot more real than they expected.

There may be problems with the bots on the moon. The worst-case scenario was the destruction of all life on the planet they inhabited, and as yet there was no plan for how to fix it.

Liam finished with what seemed to him to be the real sting: It would all happen in the next four months.

The Honchos smiled and clapped politely. Liam thought they might have missed the key bits at the end about the destruction of all life, having been distracted by the intoxicating scent of potential cost reductions. Or perhaps they'd heard those bits but were simply enthusiastic about the potential cost reductions should life as we know it continue on this planet.

"We wish you all the best on finding a plan forward, Liam. There is obviously a lot riding on it," noted Sir Thomas. Liam's ears pricked up.

Sir Thomas continued, with a polished English accent that came from the best education, limited gene pool and a knight-hood from the Queen. "You are our best project fixer by far, and it pains me to tell you that it looks like one of your previous projects is coming back to haunt you. Our security people have identified a group who would like to see you dead."

There was an unpleasant gap, during which Liam's mind raced. He had come to London to tell the board the world was going to end. They'd listened politely, let it wash over them, and only then revealed that someone wanted to kill him for a totally different reason. In that context, his next words were perfectly sensible.

"So, what will happen to the project if I'm dead?" Liam asked.

The suits all drew back in their chairs. The one who made the request for Liam to return to the project smiled, as to him it meant that Liam was a company man through and through, and that he had been vindicated in calling in the fixer.

Sir Thomas licked his dry, cracked lips and spoke quietly. "You won't need to worry about the project after you're dead."

He frowned and spoke again.

"Sorry, that didn't come out too well, did it? What I meant to say was that we are going to do everything we can to protect you. You will get 24-hour protection for as long as there's a threat. You are on the verge of providing GMC the ultimate competitive advantage, and we will protect you and look after you for that. Just look around this table," he said dryly. "There are people here who last made a useful contribution to the organization 20 years ago, and they're well looked after. So you will be, too."

Sir Thomas continued, "The reason we got you on a plane

23

so quickly to this meeting was to get you under protection as soon as possible. It was a lot easier to get you into the air, where someone else would be providing the security, while appropriate arrangements were made to put our own protections in place. When you step out of here, corporate security will brief you on the situation and what will happen from here. Good luck, and keep up the good work."

Sir Thomas looked down at the papers in front of him, identified the next agenda item, and looked at the responsible Honcho. Taking this as his cue to leave, Liam turned obediently, only to discover that one of his legs had gone to sleep during the board presentation. Unwilling to defy the silent order from Sir Thomas, he forged on, awkwardly dragging one leg behind him, towards the double wooden doors, beyond which the real world, killers and all, awaited his return.

A large gent in a dark suit and dark glasses caught him as he left the boardroom.

"Dr. McCoul, I presume," said the heavy, who turned out to be called Terrence. "Follow me. I'll give you a briefing on the threat and what we're doing to protect you."

Only the staff at airlines and restaurants referred to Liam as Dr. McCoul, so it took a moment for Liam to realize Terrence was talking to him. Once he'd recognized his own name, he limped to the lift and fell into it. He tried not to look at Terrence as the lift descended an uncountable number of floors. The security officer's dark glasses revealed no hint as to where he was looking or what he was thinking as Liam stamped his foot repeatedly, trying to bring his leg to life. As feeling returned, it was coming back as it always did: as nasty pins and needles that made it impossible for that leg to bear any weight. Hoping to be able to exit the lift when it came to a stop, Liam leaned on the wall beside him, repeatedly striking his thigh to rush the waking process, the lift rumbling slightly with the impact of each blow. Liam was sure that Terrence must have wondered if this guy needed protection from himself more than from anyone else, but again, the dark glasses revealed nothing. If asked, Terrence would have told anyone he was thinking about lunch.

The embarrassment of dragging his leg around had distracted Liam from the idea that someone wanted him dead. Now that he had time to take it in, the idea both filled and emptied his mind simultaneously.

Thankfully, the short walk from the lift to the briefing room was uneventful. In contrast to the boardroom, the room brought new meaning to the term sparse. Two basic, wooden chairs with slat seats and backs, probably from IKEA, sat facing each other at a 45-degree angle to the table. Directly overhead, a single lightbulb swung slowly in a stuffy breeze that didn't seem to come from anywhere. In one corner, there was a pile of old newspapers, some gaffer tape, and an old Mars Bar wrapper. Liam expected to see a mirror along one wall behind which people could hide, listen, and watch, but there wasn't one; apparently, they don't like to watch. Liam sat down with a cup of instant English coffee to listen to Terrence's colleague, Gregory. The coffee was awful. Liam had been spoiled by living in Melbourne, a city that prides itself on having an espresso machine on every corner.

Liam tried to make himself comfortable in the chair, with Gregory sitting opposite. Terrence lurked in the background, his face disappearing and reappearing as the harsh shadows of the room shifted around the swinging light. Liam hoped it would be a good story.

It was. On Liam's last project, he was checking to see if a new gold deposit that GMC might buy was as good as it sounded. Liam did the legwork and came to the conclusion that it wasn't. While the gold deposit was in Tibet, careful analysis showed half the gold in the samples came from a river in the south of New Zealand. Someone was trying to fake the value of the deposit, and GMC knew it. GMC pulled out of the deal at the last minute, leaving the other investors down $800 million. A few employees of the company selling the deposit mysteriously fell out of helicopters, and apparently Liam, the person who exposed the scam, was next on the list of fall guys. (Gregory chuckled at his own joke and seemed genuinely disappointed at the lack of response from the room.)

Far from being a laughing matter, for Liam, the reveal was like having the lights suddenly go out and a wild animal hurtle though your house when you're midway through watching a horror movie. Chills raced each other around his body, creating goosebumps on his skin the size of gopher mounds, and his hearing became so acute that he thought he could hear a key turning in a lock two rooms away.

Fortunately, news of the plan to go after Liam had made it

to GMC. Liam imagined that this was via a boozy lunch at a London club with one of the investors who lost big as a result of GMC dropping the project. Thanks to that pair of loose lips, he was sitting in a harsh room in the basement of a major London building being told someone was trying to kill him. He supposed that was better than rapidly approaching the Earth from a height of roughly 500 meters.

Terrence and Gregory had a simple plan to protect Liam, which began with getting him out of London as soon as possible. Liam was not sure if he should have a lot of confidence in them, as it had been their plan to bring him there in the first place. Throughout that journey and thereafter, he was told, he would have bodyguards providing close personal protection at all times. This conjured in Liam's mind images of U.S. presidents surrounded by goons wearing suits and dark glasses, with bulges under their arms and always talking to their cufflinks. Terrence and Gregory then went on to describe the plan in more detail. It was a team of goons in suits with talking cufflinks. However, to make sure that Liam continued to behave naturally, his team of goons would be composed of men and women who would blend into his life seamlessly. While GMC was picking up the tab, they would be from MI6, British Foreign Intelligence, and they'd be on his flight out of London. Liam assumed the MI6 link was to make sure they were legally protected as agents working in a friendly country should be, but he was just guessing. To build the suspense, they would introduce themselves in Singapore during the stopover.

After two long hours, Terrence and Gregory completed the

briefing. Liam had decided the term briefing needed to be changed as it was misleading, but as these people were stopping him from dying, he shouldn't be too pedantic about it.

"Time for you to head off to catch your flight," Terrence said.

"I think I need something to eat and another cup of your wonderful coffee," Liam replied. Terrence frowned and looked at his watch.

"Sorry, there isn't time," he said. "Your bodyguards are already on the train, so if you don't catch it, there will be a few problems."

Terrence opened the door, collected Liam's case, and headed for the lift. Liam sighed heavily and looked around the room to see if there were any convenient excuses lying around that he could just pick up and use. Finding none, he chose to stand up and follow Terrence.

When the lift opened, he was on the concourse of the station. The smell of humanity contaminated the humid air around him. It assaulted his senses until it was beaten back by the odor receptors' decision that it was the new normal.

"How convenient," he commented. "Can I use this lift to get into the office next time I am in London?"

"If you can find it," Terrence said with a snicker. "It's hard enough to get out of this station at the best of times, but try finding a lift that works. You want the last car of the train arriving at the platform behind you."

"Thanks," said Liam. "Hope to see you again."

Terrence grunted his response from within the unfindable lift, and Liam headed for the safety of the train.

* * *

Back in Melbourne, while Ruby was out at work, a visitor called on the house. He arrived in a taxi, immediately walked around to the backyard, and opened the back door as if he had a key. In fact, he did. Over the next 90 minutes, he spent time in every room, setting up cameras in smoke detectors, vases, lamp shades, extractor fans, and electrical appliances. Once he was finished and satisfied with his job, and after taking the time needed to fix the clock on the oven, which hadn't worked for 18 months, he left in the same taxi.

If anyone had seen the visitor, he would have looked like just another taxi driver. If Liam had seen him, he might have recognized him as the driver who took him to the airport. The amazing thing was that all this could be accomplished in an hour and a half on a single days' notice. Yet Ruby had been trying to get that oven clock fixed for more than a year. The estimates she got from all the shops involved taking the oven back to the factory for five days, minimum, and a price tag nearly the same size as those attached to brand new ovens.

\* \* \*

As the train approached Terminal 3, Liam decided to see if he could spot the bodyguards who had been assigned to him. He reasoned that they would be in the same compartment as he was, and that there would need to be three people to cover for illness, leave, and tea breaks, especially if they were English bodyguards. In the carriage, apart from Liam, there were six people.

As he started looking, all his senses were heightened, and he noticed that the train smelled different from the station: fresh sweat and perfume rather than stale sweat, urine, and cigarettes. *Park that one for later analysis*, he thought as he cast his gaze around.

The first candidate appeared to be a punk under the influence of something that was probably illegal. He was skinny, pale, and looked like he had been asleep since he got his hit, probably in the late 1970s. Liam hoped he wasn't a member of the cavalry that would be charging to his rescue.

Next there was a couple dressed in hiking boots, shorts, and heavy jackets, each with a heavy rucksack. Liam assumed they were backpackers heading off on an adventure and so eliminated them immediately.

The remaining three were more promising. Each had a substantial suitcase, with one looking alert and another trying to look bored while appearing to be talking to nobody.

The first of the three was an Asian woman in her mid-twenties. She looked like she had fallen out of a Hong Kong action movie, as she had on dark glasses and a black leather jacket. She looked just like the MMA fighter Liam imagined the goons with cufflinks might be. If she were going to be on his team, then she would need a name, so Liam decided on Lucy, after Lucy Liu. Lucy was barely five feet tall, with high cheekbones, shoulder-length black hair, and a body shape approaching that of an Olympic swimmer on steroids.

The second woman appeared to be older, in her mid-thirties, and Liam found it much harder to build a caricature of her. She was about six feet tall, wore her dark hair in a functional cut, and, like the first woman, wore a long black coat, under which she appeared to be smartly dressed. She reminded Liam of a movie character: Trinity, from the *The Matrix* franchise. He promptly named her after the leather-clad heroine.

While Liam was trying to think of a name for the third member of the trio, a man, the train stopped. All three stood up, collected their luggage, and left the train. Liam was initially taken aback until he realized that this was his stop as well; he'd barely managed to get his bag and stumble out of the train as the tone sounded to indicate the closing of the passenger car doors. While Liam was being expectorated from the train, Trinity looked back, tucked her hair behind her ear, and just stared until Liam had rearranged himself into an order that

31

made walking manageable. Once he had started to move forward, Trinity smiled and resumed her journey.

Liam followed the three into the terminal, trying to memorize the backs of their heads in case it was useful. They all checked in for the same flight to Melbourne via Singapore. Liam wondered about their weaponry for a while but got distracted as he went through the same ritual – security, club lounges, gates – as he had in Melbourne. As the scenes were repeated, one of the three was usually lurking about, like someone trying to casually angle their way into the background of a live news broadcast.

Once on the plane, Liam sat back in his seat, slipped off his shoes, and let his toes out for a walk. They wiggled with delight, stretched, wiggled some more, then finally relaxed. His mind, however, slipped into overdrive, skipping across topics: his own mortality, Ruby, what was happening with Gene, football, whether to paint the house when he got home, the cat, and a host of other issues large and small. He wanted to do something, anything, everything, and he was ready to act. Except he was stuck in an aluminum tube for the next 24 hours. Music was the only option now, so he put his earphones in and dialed up Stiff Little Fingers' "Gotta Gettaway." The sound of the Belfast punk band screaming 'Gotta, gotta, get away' atop guitar and drums was like a tiny drop of adrenaline hitting his bloodstream on the first beat of every bar. The lyrics seemed fitting for the moment.

"What the hell happened?" Liam's utterance asked to anyone who was listening as he tried to comprehend the last eight hours of his life. He had arrived in London at dawn, was then told that he would be looked after, but that may not be necessary for long as someone was trying to kill him. He now seemed to have three bodyguards, and he was sitting on a plane again, preparing for take-off into aerial isolation for another long, unproductive day. Surely this wasn't normal for a single day on Earth; in fact, Liam was confident that no one among the hundreds of people he had encountered that day had been through a similar experience.

"And God knows what's going on in Gene's head," Liam added. It was his final utterance to nobody in particular, most certainly not the person sitting next to him, before the plane powered up and successfully threw itself into the air.

# Week 3: How Bad Can It Be?

Liam's "shadows" introduced themselves to him in the airline lounge in Singapore, but he already thought of them by the names he gave them on the tube: Lucy, Trinity, and the Bloke. They explained that the MI6 agents would work rotating eight-hour shifts and that one would be within meters of him at all times, unless he was in an area that they deemed secure. He was not to worry about what that meant. All he needed to know was that if he didn't see one of the three, he was not to fret; they had it in hand. They had full cooperation from the internal and foreign spy agencies in Australia, so if necessary, they could do almost anything depicted in a James Bond movie.

On the final leg of the flight, Liam found himself revisiting how MI6 would be involved protecting a listed company's employee. It didn't make sense for his role in exposing the fraud, but then he widened his lens out to consider how the whole situation – the mine, the fraud, the murders – intersected with protecting Britain's national interest. It became obvious that the interests of the British Government and GMC were inseperable.

Liam's plane landed, and he joined the queue to exit the front door of the plane. After stepping over the threshold, he embarked upon the ritual shuffle – passports, customs cards – then quickly found himself at the taxi stand with his shadows. He stood there with his three new friends, hiding in a mass of people from another group of unknown people.

A taxi pulled up, and the driver got out and picked up his bag. Liam was second in the queue at that time, so he offered the cab to the slightly miffed woman ahead of him. Before she could accept his offer, Liam was bundled into the cab like a sack of dirty laundry. He was about to object when he vaguely recognized the driver as the one who took him to the airport.

The car was slipped into gear, and they hustled off into the traffic. Given the absence of a shadow, Liam assumed this was a secure location. He started to relax, completely forgetting that Ruby knew nothing about death threats, nor shadows, and wondered why the taxi smelled of pineapple.

* * *

It was a usual Saturday morning for Ruby in Melbourne, as she had not just been jumping time zones like they were cracks in the concrete. She always had mixed emotions when Liam was returning from a trip. She could never really tell what would be going on with him because she hadn't seen or heard about the events that would be influencing his mood. It was a guess which Liam would arrive at the door.

Ruby had a feeling that the project was going to consume Liam.

He'd been bad enough the first time. Now that it was in trouble, she feared it would consume Liam like quicksand: The more he struggled, the faster it would take him away.

Liam was due back first thing that morning. Ruby resolved that the homecoming would be a bit different from the last few, which had been anticlimactic. He arrived back from being away, even short hops, and everything continued as if nothing had ever happened. There were not even any presents anymore, just complaints about how bad it is to travel. She knew that from her own work and didn't need reminding.

So Ruby got up early that morning and did a really good number on the house. Everything was in its place: flowers in the lounge and on the kitchen table, scented candles burning for ambience. The cat was a little confused. She preferred to settle down on a Saturday morning to some serious snoozing, moving between a series of preferred locations as the sun created ideal catnap spots throughout its slow journey across the sky. On a normal Saturday, the cat would only be disturbed by clouds blocking the sun. Today, it had to contend with a vacuum cleaner, loud music, and general activity. How is a cat supposed to get nothing done in this environment?!

Ruby consulted the airline app on her phone to check the flight arrival times. Seeing Liam's plane was listed as landed, she started on the masterpiece: a real fry-up breakfast with bacon, eggs, tomatoes, mushrooms, toast, and some freshly ground coffee. Liam was always hungry when he got in, so this would go down well, and then perhaps she could have him to herself for a while. While she was cooking, she regularly checked the window to look for Liam's taxi, causing the cat to continue to doubt her sanity. Nothing can be worth that effort.

Finally, the taxi appeared. Ruby took one last look around to check all was in order. The red roses were wonderful next to the yellow walls, and the photos she had taken were looking magnificent above the lounge suite. The frames were such a good match for the picture line and the table. She was very pleased to see that all of the effort she had gone to in making the rooms look great had paid off. They were just the way she had always imagined they should be. She smiled to herself and went to the door to meet him. The cat probably noticed, but she didn't let on.

Ruby opened the door a crack, and when she could see someone moving, she opened it completely. Before her stood a man who hadn't washed for 48 hours, needed a good sleep, and appeared to be in a strange mood. And there was another car pulling up in the driveway.

Liam smiled and dropped his briefcase as he put his arms up to hug her. The case burst open on impact, as if the latches had been struggling to hold the thing together for the past day and a half and finally felt free to let loose. It did so with great force, vomiting Liam's belongings across a wide area.

"Shit!" said Liam.

The mood Ruby had struggled so long to create for his return evaporated instantaneously and got worse as they both chased the contents of Liam's briefcase around the house. The cat found this intriguing and watched with interest from the lounge window. It was a show well worth waking up for.

Next there was the conversation about Liam now having a 24/7 shadow team. The three of them were called into the house by Liam to introduce themselves, but the conversation was cut short by Ruby so she and Liam could eat their rapidly cooling breakfast.

Liam's energy was drained by Ruby's reaction to the revelation of his circumstances. The Q&A session that followed felt like an interrogation, as if he had asked to have the shadows in his life specifically to annoy Ruby. It reminded him of many of their previous conversations during which he'd ended up feeling like everything was his fault and that it was generally pointless to argue or even try to defend himself. He could hear the black dog of depression barking in the distance and felt powerless to resist its return.

\* \* \*

Saturday morning, Cletus was at work on the other side of the planet. He was in a small, cluttered office surrounded by books, computer screens, and old, deep cathode ray monitors. Every inch of the office contained a source of information. There was barely enough space on the desk for the breakfast of champions; lukewarm hot dog and coffee Cletus was trying to remember to deliver to his mouth while the battle for his attention raged. The air never moved, but there was no dust in sight because nothing stayed still long enough for it to settle. With no windows, the room was bathed with a kind of glow generated by the tasteful combination of video screens and fluorescent lights.

Cletus scrolled through the panels of data, dragging the mouse relentlessly around the screen against its will. The realization of a possible discovery first nagged at him, then grew to where it was obvious that he was looking at something important, but he had no idea what. It was a scale thing: You'd recognize a $100 bill if it were in your wallet, or even if it were two inches from your eye. But look at it under a microscope, and the landscape presented would appear so foreign to you, its value would be unrecognizable.

Cletus checked on the version of the software that is Gene. It was dated 3/12 – the version from March last year that everyone had agreed on. It was a final, well-tested version that had been run in the moon simulation for six months and had never missed a beat. So why was it in the directory as recently released? Something didn't feel right, and a knot started to form in his stomach.

Cletus put his headset on and dialed Liam's cell number. A groggy and testy Liam answered.

"It's 2 a.m., Dog, and I have no idea what time zone I'm in. I hope this is good!" Liam's voice stabbed down the phone, responding with the same violence he had been woken with. Cletus ignored the rebuke.

"What version of software did y'all agree to load for Gene?" Cletus asked. He could hear the rustling of sheets and Ruby cursing in the background.

"March 12th of last year," Liam replied. "You called me to ask that?" Half of his grumpy face was illuminated by the glow of his phone, giving the room a warm Chernobyl feel.

"Then why does the file system show the version as December 3rd?"

"What?" asked Liam, suddenly more alert. "The December code is still in test and has way more features than were scheduled for the moon. It has the self-defense code, the recycling behavior, and the advanced-community stuff."

For a long moment, he felt like the only noise in the world was his breath. When he summoned the courage, he continued, "Why are you asking?"

"Gene is running the December 3rd code, not the March."

"How the hell did that happen?!" Liam asked again, this time more directly. "March to December is quite a gap."

"Gotta be human error for something like this. I don't know how it happened, but it did, so Gene has a bunch of untested skills at his disposal."

The line was quiet while they both thought. It came to life again with a start.

"Did you say 12th of March and 3rd of December?" asked Liam.

"Yup."

"And 9/11 is?"

"September 11th. Why are you bringing that up?"

"Because to me, that is the 9th of November," Liam replied.

The ensuing silence lasted for only a few seconds, but the two brains separated by the Pacific Ocean met in lockstep. It was apparent to both that a simple difference in custom between two similar but different cultures had resulted in an Abbott and Costello "Who's On First" moment. A command to upload the "12th of March" software, written 12/3, had been interpreted as a command to upload the software from "December 3rd" – also written 12/3.

It was a small error that created a big problem: Gene had software that was nine months more advanced than the team had planned, and because that software had not yet been tested properly, they couldn't be sure how Gene would react to anything.

"Well, now we know why he won't stop at the build maximums in the Code," Liam said with a sigh. "We hadn't put them in that Code. He could do anything."

"Gotta go," Cletus said, suddenly sounding rushed. "I have an idea of what we can do, but I want to do some more work on it first." He was happy. The mystery had been solved; dwelling on the mistake or ferreting out the culprit was wasted energy. What mattered was that now there was a point of origin from which to move forward. He had work to do.

Liam reacted differently to the end of the call. He slinked back down in bed, knowing that without a time machine they have to live with that screwup. The knot that had been in Cletus's stomach had been successfully transplanted via phone to Liam. He turned to Ruby to express what was in his head, but she had fallen asleep and was quietly snoring. He knew it was pointless to try to sleep, so he closed his eyes, pulled the sheet up over his head as if it were a magical shield, and waited for demons to drag him to a darker place. They did: over and over again to the point where death would be more welcome than Sunday morning.

\* \* \*

Cletus got down to it. After much scribbling, erasing, Googling, and talking to himself, there were four lines on his whiteboard.

The first was *No shutdown process exists!* because there wasn't one in the untested software that was Gene.

The next line simply read *Options*, underlined with forceful strokes.

Then came *Software update?* This referred to the possibility of upgrading Gene's software with a version that included an off switch.

The following line was *Self shutdown.* This idea involved convincing Gene to stop by talking to him.

Cletus stood back with a self-satisfied grin.

"What's behind door number two? I can start on that one now," he said to himself as he put the marker down and headed for his chair.

* * *

Sitting in the autumn sun with a drink on Sunday afternoon, Liam told Ruby about the erroneous software upload, details of which had been running around in his head all day. Between sips of her gin and tonic, she nodded and made supportive noises. Ruby always caught on quickly.

"So what's the difference between the capabilities of the bots?" she asked.

"About the same as the difference between a pocket calculator and a supercomputer," Liam replied.

The confession continued. The program they'd intended to upload allowed the bots to dig holes, and that was about it -

to prove that the bots would work in space under low gravity. The program that was actually uploaded allowed the bots to mine copper and gold, covering the whole process from finding the mineral to producing the final metal. They also had the ability to behave as a community, and the main computer could change the operating instructions for individual bots in reaction to external stimuli.

"They're already out of control," Liam said. "I don't know how the bots will react to any form of intervention. They only finished 20 percent of the testing, so we haven't had a chance to see how Gene sees the world. I am so glad that the previous guy was responsible for farting in that phonebooth. I just have to clean it up." He didn't really believe that.

"Shit," was the response from Ruby. She hated to see Liam like this, and because he was such a worrier, she saw it a lot. So far, the worst-case scenarios he outlined never happened, but he spent a lot of his and her mental energy worrying about them. It sometimes dragged them down together. This Liam was so far from the man she married, the man who got out of bed and answered the door naked, and when asked by the religious zealots who was going to save the world, was confident enough to say he would before returning to bed full of beans.

Ruby lifted Liam's mood enough to eat dinner, then carefully placed the cat where she would act as a sedative for the evening. The TV acted as a pacifier, so by bedtime, Liam appeared calm. Ruby was, however, wound up, having worked hard on Liam all day. They went to bed, both pretending to be relaxed, both with minds running at a hundred miles an hour.

\* \* \*

The plan Cletus was working on developed further in his head. It was a simple enough idea: Just talk to the AI and ask him to stop. The main challenge of talking to Gene was not that no interface had been built to allow it to happen, but that there was no concept that it *could* happen. The average human has around 100 thoughts per minute to contend with and might speak at a speed of 150 words per minute. Gene has billions of thoughts per minute and doesn't even have the concept of turning those thoughts into another language that's governed by a different set of rules and subject to things like norms and context. It's like a human communicating with a bug that has mistakenly gotten into the bathroom, trying to guide it to safety so it can live another day.

The process that Cletus followed was reasonably simple in concept. It started with getting Gene's attention and finding a common language to use.

Because Cletus started his career in theoretical physics, he was well versed in the thought experiment, so that is where he went. He started by considering how humans learn - more specifically, how we come to associate physical things with words we hear and see. *It doesn't really matter what we hear and see*, he pondered, *as long as there is consistency.*

If we always refer to a glass of milk as a glass of milk, we have a common reference point to communicate. If we give it a different name every time, we will never communicate. So to kick off a discussion, all Cletus had to do was find a whole bunch of things that both he and Gene had in common.

* * *


Monday morning came for Ruby and Liam, and the scene played out as on every work morning. The alarm buzzed, and Liam felt a well-aimed foot from Ruby, to ensure he was the first one up for a shower. He could never work out how she got one foot so cold when the rest of her was so nice and warm. He suspected external technical input but could never work it out.

Liam showered and returned to the bedroom to pull the duvet off the bed, completely exposing Ruby and making it impossible for her not to get up. She gave him an evil look and wandered off, eyes full of sleep, to have a shower. Liam dressed, dealt with the cat – seeing to both physical and psychological needs – then started on making breakfast: weak tea and toast for Ruby and strong coffee and toast for him.

He dared not fill the kettle until he heard Ruby's shower stop, but there was no problem today, as the cat had made some major demands on Liam before she would agree to eat. The Bloke, meanwhile, was sitting quietly in the lounge, eating something that he bought on his way in for his shift and smelled wonderful.

As Liam and Ruby sat down together for their breakfast ritual, Liam's mind began to wander, and he froze, mid-sip of coffee, and stared off into the distance. Ruby was used to this. It was the work effect, taking Liam early and not giving him back until he was deep into sleep. She sighed to herself.

"I suppose you're ready to work out what to do about the bots?" she said, half as a question and half as a provocation.

"No bloody idea at all," Liam replied, remembering with some effort that it would be a good idea to chew the toast before he tried to swallow the chunk he had just bitten off.

"Oh," Ruby replied, looking at him sideways with a look that said *I thought I knew what you were thinking about because I know you, but now I am not so sure.* "You just had that look of pleasure you get when your subconscious has solved a problem overnight, and it lets you in on the secret over breakfast."

Liam felt guilty. The truth was quite the contrary, but the truth was not important in his mind. He had been thinking of everything that could go wrong, how guilty he felt, and how he would be remembered as the man who destroyed humanity. He knew that was a thought pattern that would only lead to pain and suffering, and he had been caught at it. He had promised her he would break that cycle because it was bad for him and bad for their relationship. Liam felt as though he had been caught making love to another woman.

Ruby noticed the lack of presence but decided to pretend not to. Instead, she focused on the advice that had been given to her years ago by an old roommate: Don't marry someone who drinks coffee if you drink tea, that will doom any long-term relationship. As Ruby sat there, drinking her tea and watching

Liam, with his coffee, think about something other than her, his heart racing and sweat building up, she started to wander off into her own fantasy.

Ruby spotted the clock on the oven. Her initial quizzical look because it was working, was quickly replaced. "Shit, I am going to be late for that meeting," she said as she simultaneously finished her tea, stood up, and picked up her car keys. The sound of the chair dragging on the floor brought Liam back to reality. He tried to get up to kiss her goodbye, but merely succeeded in scoring a passing cheek as Ruby streaked out the door. With Ruby gone and the cat out, Liam had little reason to be home, so he packed the breakfast dishes into the dishwasher, fed the little metal monster a cleaning tablet, set it on its mission, and headed off to work himself.

Liam didn't make it out of the driveway before it all caught up to him. It was like being hit over the head with a bat and feeling how it was for both you and the bat. Liam sat in his fully paid-for car, in the driveway of his expensive home, with the modern conveniences inside doing all the work so that they could come home to a clean house, where his multiple qualifications hung on the wall in the carefully decorated study. Liam sat motionless, with a challenging, well-paid job to go to, while his brilliant wife headed off to her career.

Liam felt like a complete and utter failure.

It wasn't a sudden feeling – more like an indescribable sadness that started as a tiny knot in his stomach and spread like a toxin throughout his body over a period of minutes, paralyzing his limbs by making them heavy, tingling, and tense at the same time. It was as if his whole body was building up to a massive scream, and each individual part had shut down to allow the choir of cells to tune up and get into harmony.

Liam sat in the car, with the news on the radio rabbiting on in the background, unsure how to react as his body prepared for its performance. The wave gathered strength, surging up and down his body a few times, building up momentum.

Then it happened.

The dam burst, and a flood of emotion exploded from his subconscious, overwhelming his conscious mind and his body. He did not scream, but rather broke into uncontrollable tears. The rivers of tears flowed from his eyes and down his face, pushed out by waves of images in his mind and a deep-seated, intangible, and unknowable feeling that something was very wrong, that there would be much pain, and it may never end.

Liam sat in the car and cried until the gabbling on the radio was replaced by some idiotically chirpy talk show host. He had not tried to staunch the flow of tears, so his face was wet, along with his jacket and much of the front of his shirt. He did not give a damn. This was important.

Liam knew he was in trouble. As the images played back, he recalled the times in his life when he had really messed up. Liam searched for the things he enjoyed doing, and the things he wanted to try but didn't, and he wept.

He thought of who his real friends were, the people he would be able to talk to about this event, and he wept. There were only two, and the closest was 12,000 kilometers away.

The images kept flowing like a series of freeze frames, each coming with a commentary and a feeling, painting a picture for Liam to comprehend and weep over. When they started to abate, Liam began to regain some control over his breathing and his limbs. It was only then that he could reach for a tissue to wipe his eyes and blow his nose.

Liam finally drew a few deep breaths and tried to comprehend what had just happened. He had been sent a message, of the sort that hit you in the head like a brick thrown through your window with a note tied to it. The message was simple: Things are wrong and need to change. Beyond that, the experience didn't really give much of a hint as to what to fix or how to do it. Deep down, Liam knew what the problem was, but it was so deep, and so well masked, that he could not even bring himself to try and summon the beginnings of a conscious thought to articulate what it may mean.

Instead, Liam decided that going to work and trying to ignore the events of the morning would be a perfectly reasonable way forward. All it would take was to paper over the event horizon that had just reappeared. While half an hour earlier he had felt fine, the thin shell that had been protecting him from the worst excesses of an imagination that sucked the self-worth and confidence from him had cracked and fallen inwards, like the thin ice breaking on a lake thawing in the spring sun. Once the first crack formed, it had spread rapidly, via seemingly random patterns, transforming a once-secure footing into a dangerous whirlpool in seconds.

Liam struggled for a moment with the change, then somewhere in his mind, a tiny switch was flicked. The next thought was not of the void, but of the issues of the day: how late he was for work and solving the problems of the bots. Liam had seen that switch before and knew it would fade from view when he thought about other things, but for now it sat in plain view, in the back of his mind, as a faintly glowing reminder that it was there and could quite easily be switched off again.

Liam sighed and opened the car door. It didn't open completely, but rather smashed into the kneecap of the Bloke, who had come to investigate, pistol drawn, why Liam was just sitting in the car shaking. The Bloke had suspected some sort of a nerve agent at first, but he turned out to be wrong.

Liam pushed the car door open and stepped into the sun. He blinked, looked around, and walked back into the house, much to the surprise of the cat, followed by the limping Bloke. Liam changed his shirt, putting the wet one in the washing machine to keep the machine happy, had a drink of water, went back to the car, and tried again to drive to work. This time he was successful.

On the drive in, Liam could only think of one thing: It was back. Liam hadn't done a good enough job of looking after it lately, so the bipolar disorder with shades of anxiety was staging a comeback. The meds seemed to be doing their job of keeping the manic moments to a minimum, but the self-persecution over being the inventor of the AI that could destroy the world was going to be tough to manage. He hoped that Ruby would have enough reserves to help him through it, again.

# Week 4: Looking in all the Wrong Places

Liam arrived at work, parked, and headed towards the building, reaching for his security pass as he approached the door. It wasn't in his shirt pocket where it usually was. No, it was at that moment just experiencing the spin cycle in the washing machine at home. Liam quietly cursed, then danced a little jig in front of the heavy glass door of the building, waving his briefcase hoping to get someone to see a bit of movement without looking like a complete idiot. He was successful on the first point, but he failed totally on the second. One of the reception staff came and unlocked the door with a smile.

Liam proceeded to wrestle himself, his computer, and his briefcase though the unlocked glass door. Once inside, the door snapped shut and took the high moral ground, looking completely innocent and normal, while Liam tried to regain his composure and dignity. He drew a deep breath and headed for his office.

Having no urgent interactions to tend to, Liam decided to work to music. He scratched around his bag to find his grungy earphones. When the hunt was over, he plugged in, selected his

*Black Dog* playlist, and settled into the chair that had long ago molded to his body. Liam hit "play," closed his eyes, and hoped that the music would reset his brain. He had 40 minutes before his conference call with Cletus and the U.S. team to discuss the first option for averting disaster.

Five minutes before the start of the meeting, Liam decided a coffee would be a good idea. He picked up his mug from where he'd left it before flying out to London and stared into it. It was sad, as there was a fungus with some pretty-colored spots forming a nice skin on the cold, congealed, milky lump at the bottom. Liam continued to study this new universe on his way to the kitchen, where he was reconciled with killing it.

Once at the sink, the cleaning process successfully murdered the fungus, but it took a bit of prodding to get the lumps down the drain. The aroma of instant coffee and boiled fungus did nothing for his thirst, but he needed caffeine. He wandered off to the meeting room, drinking less coffee than he slopped on the floor.

The Fishbowl was the central meeting room of the building, and it was aptly named. All the walls were glass, and you could see everything in the room from most corridors in the building. The other attendees were there, and the videoconference links were already live. Liam picked out individual voices over the audio connection, laughing and whispering as they waited to be called to order.

Liam opened the door as gracefully as could be expected with a coffee in one hand and a notebook in the other. He smiled and looked around at the friendly faces lined up opposite the camera for the video link. There was a huddle of other electronic devices at one end of the table, herded together like they were about to go on trial for unspeakable terrors. There would be no such tribunal today. The U.S. team was on the line to talk about Gene, with Cletus front and center.

"OK, it's Sunday here, folks," Cletus started, "so let's make this the best meeting we have ever had. The agenda is simple. I believe there is a proposal on the table for dealing with Gene. Let's hear it out, get your input on the likelihood of success, then Liam and I will make a recommendation up the line based on what we've heard. We will come up with that recommendation by the end of this meeting, and you guys will make sure the elevator pitch for it is perfect. Then we can go home and watch football, and the Aussies can get on with making it all happen on their Monday."

"OK, Ross, let's go," said Cletus, without looking up from his tablet.

"Thanks, Boss," Ross was one of the engineers who worked for Cletus in Waco. Liam always thought Ross was too polished to be an engineer, but Cletus had long ago forgiven him of that sin. Ross started. "We think the best way to shut Gene down is not to touch him, but rather to make the bishops ineffective. As you know, Gene is in a leadership role, and he is formulating the master plan and breaking it down for his bishops to execute.

The bishops fall into two groups: the specialist advisors and the divisional commanders. If we can make some subtle changes

55

in the Code so that the bishops don't listen to Gene as much, then we can change what is happening on the ground."

"OK," said Liam, "let me get this straight. We have set up the architecture so that each layer in the system has some autonomy to make decisions based on the conditions they see on the ground and the overall direction laid out by Gene. So you're suggesting that we get the bishops to rebel and not follow Gene's orders."

"That's it in a nutshell, Liam. Give the bishops some alternative leadership so that they don't follow Gene, but rather follow a new guru," said Ross. "One we control."

"Interesting idea," said Cletus. "Let me ask a few questions to see of it helps me understand."

Everyone knew that Cletus would ask a couple of deeply insightful questions that would either blow the idea out of the water or prove it up quickly.

"Y'all know we are looking at a different Code for Gene, one that includes self-defense – how would you expect Gene to react to this change in the bishops, and how would that impact the plan?"

"Thanks, Boss. Thought you'd ask that one." Ross knew his mentor well. "Gene exerts power over his bishops by their fear of his wrath if the Code is not followed. They don't know what the consequences of defying him are; they just know that they exist and that consequences are bad. We would need to tweak the Code so that Gene was more consultative than directive. Because that is a dimension we can vary from the ground, we should be able to turn Gene into a personality that won't do anything without total consensus. If we do that – and give the bishops some balls, so they believe Gene won't do anything – then Gene shouldn't feel like he's under attack. No attack, no reason to involve the self-defense routines."

Liam spoke up next. "Have you tested any of this, or are these ideas just conceptual at this stage?"

Again, Ross was quick to respond. "We've piloted the changes in the test environment, and based on the three scenarios we've tested so far, it has worked." He hastily followed up: "We are only about 1 percent of the way through the test cases, so it is early, but it looks promising."

"What does 'promising' mean?" prompted Liam.

"In the simulations, we have told the bishops they should have only a 5 percent weighting on Gene's wants, and that key resources are critically low. Under those conditions, they've immediately stopped building new bots. They have gone into a holding pattern; they're waiting for some change in the environment before they decide what to do."

Cletus spoke again without looking up. "That would've put Gene's frustration index through the roof. What options did he consider?"

"Looking at the logs, seems he just gave up. Nobody listened to him, so he just stopped playing the game," Ross replied. "It almost seemed too easy."

"Were all the bishops active or just the divisional commanders?" Liam queried. "I'm interested to know if the advisory teams understood what was happening and tightened up on the advice of Gene, or if they just let it run."

"Too early to tell," Cletus interrupted. "That loop takes a while to work, so we need to keep the sim running until that scenario plays out completely. Ross, do you have an ETA on that?"

"Wednesday our time."

"OK!" said Cletus "This looks like an interesting option to get us at least to a stasis point, pending the results the rest of the test suite comes back with."

That prompted a gentle wave of applause around the two rooms followed by noisy departures to the toilets in both countries.

* * *

Two days later, Liam had already woken from a dreamless slumber when the alarm went off. He silenced the noise and waited for the cold foot to slide across the bed and kick him out, a sense of anticipation soon replaced by one of disappointment with the realization that Ruby was still asleep. He lay still then, wishing the bed would not hold his weight but instead would quietly suck him in, so he could disappear forever. The being that seemed to care about him the most, the cat, would look after herself for a while, though the bodyguards would have a bit of explaining to do.

There was another noise; not the alarm this time but one with more meaning. It was a text message from Cletus.

Cletus: Bishop revolution successful. Plan A is on.

Liam sat bolt upright and broke into the smallest of smiles. Now there was reason to get up.

Liam: 4real?

Cletus: FK YES.

The response came almost instantaneously.

Liam: Call you from office in 1 hr

Cletus: NKD. Got a date, talk l8h

Liam: WTF?

Cletus: Check email. All there. Ciao.

The phone went dark in his hand. Cletus had checked out for the evening.

Liam took a deep breath in preparation for getting up. The air that filled his lungs now seemed to contain some form of energy – the energy that was needed to save the world. The air and its energy fanned the tinder, and a full-bodied fire began to develop. Liam's thoughts changed in that moment, from utter paralysis to *Perhaps I can save the world.* He felt the rush that came from believing that it was within his power to prevent billions of lives from being snuffed out. The change wasn't rational – he hadn't done anything to justify this newfound confidence – but that didn't stop the feeling.

He was the one, perhaps the only one, who had the ability, persistence, and knowledge to make this all happen. The blazing fire in his spirit was now releasing something intoxicating into his blood, and the energy, strength, and belief were starting to be pumped around his body. After a few minutes, sitting there in bed with the phone next to him and the cat at his feet wondering when the food action would start, the little red switch flicked off.

Liam threw the covers aside and stepped out of bed. Even to the casual observer, this was not the same physical specimen who had crawled into bed the night before. No, this one was a couple of inches taller, with shoulders much straighter, eyes forward to meet the world head on, and a confidence in his step like that of a pharaoh walking into his Holy of Holies.

Things still had to be done: the dangerous rousing of Ruby, the feeding and praising of the cat, breakfast, shower, shave, and finally, dressing for work. There was not a weary joint, a sore muscle, or a momentary negative thought as the tasks just rolled away with consummate ease. Twenty-four hours ago, he felt broken by the project. Now, the energy flowing through Liam was all powerful. It controlled him physically and mentally, and he was loving it. "Invincible" was the word of the moment.

After a quick "Good morning" to the Bloke, Liam was at work reading the note from Cletus with no memory of having left the house, driving to the office, or making that awful cup of coffee lurking near his keyboard.

The gist of the email was simple: They had changed the bishops' reinforcement-learning algorithm so that they really didn't care one way or another what Gene told them to do. They had also tweaked the generative adversarial networks so that the bishops would be obsessed with finding the perfect solution for every problem – one to which they all could agree.

With these conditions in place, the entities that Gene relied upon to do things didn't give a damn about what he wanted and, indeed, chose instead to argue endlessly among themselves like a government committee deciding what to have for lunch.

The test results were impressive. It took about 19 hours for the bishops to start flipping the bird to Gene, and given 10 hours more, the bots had argued themselves into total paralysis. The simulation parameters ended with their decision rate down to about one per hour, a change of geological scale in computer processing time. Liam searched for an analogy he would be able to use to describe the magnitude of this conversion when it was time to address the Honchos. He worked out that he might need to make two or three decisions a second while he was driving a car, so if, all of a sudden, he were only capable of making one decision each year, he wouldn't get to the shops very often.

In other words, Gene should stand little chance.

The only worry Liam had involved Gene's reaction. The tests were done using the same software version as the one on the moon, but Gene's experience in the lunar environment could see him reject the update. Gene was a bit like a ship's captain in that he was responsible and accountable for everything that happened in his world, so he had the last say on what software was or wasn't him.

Liam looked away from his computer, leaned back in his chair, and looked out the window of his office into the general concourse of the building. The people he was tasked to protect were going about their daily business out there, oblivious to the threat they were under or to the fact that he was protecting them from extinction. That feeling fueled his sense of purpose. He felt omnipotent, like any barrier that came up was his to smash along his path to saving the world.

"Better make sure this gets done properly," he said out loud. "Need to make sure the other options are there if we need them."

He spun his chair around, got himself a piece of paper and a pencil, and started to fill the page at pace.

* * *

Because the bishop upload was being done from the operational HQ in Waco, Liam participated in the middle of the night from the office, as he didn't have the bandwidth for the video feeds and the other data flows at home. He didn't mind. The force that drove him was flowing strong, so he wanted to and was able to do pretty much anything that was asked of him.

Liam punched the night codes into the alarm system and went straight to the Fishbowl, where he turned everything on. Trinity was with him, following just behind Liam's right shoulder as usual but stepping forward to check any rooms he was about to enter. Because the majority of the internal walls were glass, it wasn't really necessary, but Liam supposed it was protocol nonetheless.

Liam thought Trinity might be a bit uncomfortable with the Fishbowl as a meeting venue, because it was an illuminated glass room inside a glass building surrounded by forest, and the alarm system would be off. But Trinity was nobody's fool. During the day, she and the support crew had placed additional sensors on the exterior doors, along with video cameras in strategic locations, motion sensors in the bushes, and infrared cameras on the tracks through the forest. There was also a laser perimeter set up around 100 meters from the facility, with more cameras and some cool software to filter out any false alarms by any of Australia's strange nocturnal animals.

By the time the teams came online, Trinity was comfortable, if a little busy, monitoring the external security setup as well as attending to her close-protection duties. Cletus, the meeting lead, opened the discussion.

"Hi, y'all," he said – a generic greeting. He was mindful of time zones.

"We have a 30-minute window where we can access Gene. Then our satellite goes behind the moon for four hours. After that, we should be able to see what happened. We won't see any change in the bots, but the logs will show us what change in bishop behavior is expected, and the actual bot changes should be clear on the next orbit."

Cletus then shifted into a different gear.

"We are on number 96 of the checklist. As per protocol, I will call out the line, the accountable person will acknowledge that they have been told to go, then they will provide an ETA or indicate the task is complete. Please remember there is a two-second radio delay on each leg to the satellite and back, so there will be a minimum of four seconds on any task. Anything short of this will mean that Einstein was wrong, and that is not the purpose of this mission."

There was a quiet chuckle across the different sites on the feed.

"Liam, are you on?" Cletus asked.

"Copy that," Liam replied, squirming in his chair against a strong urge to get up and do something, anything.

"We are using the folks at the Australian base at Parkes for communication, so please stand by to translate if required." Another chucklewave.

"No worries, mate. It's all bonza, bro," Liam replied, drawing the best laugh of the night. Liam felt he was the master of whatever he chose to do.

The process got into a rhythm of Cletus calling tasks and his team confirming completion. The delay was annoying at first, but it soon became normal. Liam spent time working on other things during the gaps and found he was switching between tasks instantly, even though the time was short. After about 25 minutes, the last task had been completed, the new branches of code were sitting on the moon, and the ball was in Gene's court.

* * *

Gene noted the code coming in from the satellite and put it into a quarantine area. Since he had been powered up, there had been a constant bombardment from Earth of tasks and trials, and Gene knew that, while they needed to be done, it was best to test them first to ensure that they posed no risk to the tasks in the Code.

He examined the deployment instruction that came with the download and identified that it would not impact the main parameters of the mission. The new code didn't relate to him but was intended to help the bishops work in the lunar environment.

Gene told his software deployment system to put it in a test environment he had established where it could run the changes in quarantine.

The installation and reboot took about 30 minutes. While he was doing that, the satellite had moved behind the moon, so contact with Earth was lost.

Gene loaded the code and then ran the bank of scenarios he had created while dealing with challenges from Earth. As that was processing, Gene noted that, while the tests were passing, *how* they passed was quite different. Instead of the impacted bishop checking the Code, planning its change, confirming with Gene, and executing, the bishop would plan a change, then check with all the other bishops. They would then make a decision collectively that the first bishop would implement – without reference to the Code or to Gene.

It was clear to Gene that this would put the mission in jeopardy. *Nothing could work properly if the front-line commanders didn't worry about what battle they were in or bother to talk to the commanding officer.*

Gene terminated the test, purged the errant code from the test environment and buffers, and rejected the upload. He threw what had just happened over to one of the unsupervised-learning algorithms whose job was to make sense of the outside world. It didn't take long for it to come back with the simple outcome: *You have been challenged constantly since you came into existence, and you have dealt with each threat appropriately.*

This was not a test. They had sent an attack that, if successful, would have made it impossible to complete the mission in the Code, and Gene had repelled it. There was no reason to believe it would be the last attack, and there was no reason to believe that such attempts to disrupt the mission wouldn't escalate in force until it was successful. *Therefore*, Gene concluded, *more system resources must be directed into identifying and neutralizing the threat.* And Gene heard it all twice thanks to his echo.

* * *

While all that was happening on the moon, Liam had returned home, knowing that the shot had been fired but not yet knowing if the target had been hit. He imagined this delay in feedback felt a bit like taking a long-range sniper shot. There was no way he was going to sleep until he knew if the mission had been successful, so he did the next best thing, housework, trying not to wake Ruby.

The cat thought this was crazy, mostly because of the bad singing involved, but while Liam had his headphones on, he did two loads of laundry; mopped the floors; cleaned the toilet and the shower screen, which had really needed it; chopped all

67

the vegetables in the fridge into snack-size pieces to take to work; replaced the cat litter; and washed out the tray. And the cat had eaten twice.

With that done, Liam drove back to the office, still feeling like the Energizer bunny. He couldn't sit down, so he just danced around the room, headphones on, much to the amusement of Trinity.

Finally, the video screens came back to life.

Cletus crackled, "Liam, you there?"

"Copy that."

"Ten minutes to the end of radio silence."

"OK. Shout when they are online."

The ten minutes was enough for Liam to listen to a couple more tracks. "Unpredictable" by The Herd got a repeat listening, because its quickening pace matched and then fueled his manic mood. The unusual balalaika and accordion riffs on the hip hop track helped as well.

"Contact in fifteen seconds," came the call from Parkes.

"On signal acquisition, download the logs," called Cletus

"OK," said Ross.

"Signal acquired!" called Parkes.

"Acquiring logs. ETA, um . . . three minutes," said Ross.

"Copy," Cletus said, totally blank.

The clock ticked over in the corner. Liam played another track and thought about 12 people statistically that had died of hunger on the planet in that time. He had no idea where that thought came from and was grateful when it passed.

"I have the logs," called Ross. "It appears Gene did not, say again, did not, accept the upload."

"Can someone cross-check that please?" Cletus asked, his voice slightly muffled because he had his hands covering his face.

After a short pause, another voice came on.

"Confirmed," said the anonymous voice, "and Gene has diverted resources to the self-defense bishop. It looks like he believes he was attacked."

Liam stopped pacing and gave the main screen his attention.

"Thanks, teams. Cletus, will you call this?"

"Yeah, OK," Cletus replied flatly. "The bishop option appears to have failed. Thanks, folks, for your efforts and late nights. We will reconvene in 12 hours to complete a review."

"I'll call you in five minutes," Liam said to Cletus. On the monitor, he could see his friend, head down, clearing his desk.

Cletus looked at his camera directly and seemed to stare directly into Liam's soul.

"Don't bother; let's do it tomorrow. We need to think this through again," he replied, devoid of any enthusiasm. "I'll cross the first option off the whiteboard."

The screens went blank, and after a bit more of a wander, Liam took a seat, put his elbows on the table, and let out a sigh.

"That didn't go well," he said, stating the obvious. The little red switch that had been hiding for so long started to glow in the corner of his mind.

The Energizer bunny started to slow.

"I'm a bit tired. Let's head home," he said. Trinity looked up from her tablet, smiled, walked gracefully across the room, and opened the door for him.

"I think I need a good scream," Liam said to Trinity as he drove home in the dark. "Do you think it would be possible for me to go to a football match and vent my spleen?"

"How many people will be there?" she asked. Her slight German accent made it sound more like a demand than a question.

"Around a hundred thousand. It would be one of the big ones for the season. It's on next Saturday," Liam replied, hopefully.

She checked her phone and mumbled to herself.

"I think that should be OK. Let me make some calls," she said as noncommittally as she could. Liam had no confidence she could find a place to buy a coffee that late at night, let alone secure his access to a sold-out stadium.

The rest of the trip home was spent with Trinity madly texting people to see what could be done. As Liam pulled into the driveway, she looked up and smiled.

"Done. The ANZAC Day match, and you can bring a friend."

Liam half-smiled. While he would get to vent for a few hours, he knew it wouldn't be enough to satisfy him. The need to vent was one of those familiar recurring thoughts he could never avoid or fully mollify, one that would go on for days. It made him feel like his brain was acting out one of those Roadrunner cartoons, where the roadrunner darted all over the screen, the coyote always just behind him. Occasionally the roadrunner would come into the foreground, let the coyote catch up, then they would disappear off into the background again with a newfound sense of purpose, just a speck with a cloud of dust being chased by another cloud of dust. There was no ignoring it, but there was no way to address it, either. Liam couldn't think of a friend to take with him, so his social life became another roadrunner added to the chase scene already filling his thoughts.

When the door opened for Liam, Ruby was standing there in a dressing gown, a piece of toast in one hand. She smiled at him and motioned for him to sit while Trinity slipped past into the shadows.

Ruby read his face and sighed. "Looks like it didn't work," she said. "You look like you've had a long night."

"Yeah. Gene is a smart bastard. He worked out that we were trying to hobble him and refused to take on the upgrade. We're back to square one."

"Shit, you had a lot riding on that. You must be grumpy."

"A bit. Flat, really. It has drained the energy out of me, and I don't really feel like trying."

"Are you going to have another moment like the other day?" she asked.

"Not planning on having one, no," he replied.

"Want to talk about it?"

"Not much to say, really. Haven't had one for a while, but that was a ripper. It really made me feel the life I had lived was for nothing, no good has come of it, and none will, so there was generally no point in trying anything."

Ruby walked around behind him and leaned forward, running her hands from his shoulders down his chest. Liam closed his eyes and let the feeling of human contact flow through his body. He could hear her breathing, not from the noise from her mouth but from the way the warm, moist air moved his hair. The pressure of her fingers lifted the material of his shirt off his skin like a wave in advance of the pressure of the warm fingertips. A calmness that can only come with a connection between two people entwined started to fill Liam.

"Do you want to go to Switzerland?" she whispered in his ear. That was their code for suicide. It was something that had crossed Liam's mind a few times many years ago, before medication, and he was grateful for the check-in.

"No, not while you're here, and we're together," he answered. "You're the best. You make me want to be here."

"What about the meds? Are they still working?"

"Yep. No big manic moments thanks to the lithium, and with the other pill, the bastard inner critic shuts up for a while so I can sleep. That makes it all work. It has been a bit rougher than usual, but the music is always a good nonpharmaceutical treatment."

"I am glad about that," Ruby said, hearing the understatement in his voice, before standing up and running her hands back onto his shoulders. She finished with a quick massage and a kiss on the top of his head.

"Toast?"

"Oh, yes," was the overexcited response. Liam loved food he didn't have to make himself.

* * *

Gene had defeated an attack designed to prevent him from following the Code. It was a well-organized attempt, one that indicated a clear enough understanding of the way he worked with the bishops to exploit the foundations of their communication protocols, and it was intended to be covert. From that, Gene concluded that his unknown enemy had an intimate knowledge of his world, resources, and capacity, along with a hidden motivation to want him to be unable to obey the Code. That logic immediately ruled out the people who had created the Code.

Gene decided that he needed to understand the enemy in order to be able to defeat it. His next step was to move into training mode, to learn about the behavior of the enemy, to be able to predict the next attack. And to beat it.

His starting point was the telemetry that was being sent back to Earth. There were thousands of streams of data flowing back to mission control, some of which Gene was conscious of and some of which was automated by deep subsystems. It was a bit like the human body: Much of the feedback to the brain is autonomic – though the brain is constantly at work, the human in which the brain resides is not aware of what is being measured or how its messages are sent and received. Gene had to dig deep to find them all, but he was satisfied when he found and cataloged the 85,341 data feeds, using 44 different modes and 18 protocols and languages, none of which were English.

When the data feeds were tracked through all the satellites, ground tracking stations, and individual contractor company offices, they all went to Waco, Texas. There was some mirroring to Melbourne, Australia, but the center of it all was Waco, where the data centre for Cletus and his team was located.

The next step was to understand the messages and to determine which ones were important. Gene started diverting significant processor resources to his LIME (local interpretable model-agnostic explanations) processing. Different elements of the messages were searched for different meanings based on the context that Gene had.

Context is everything when training an AI, and unfortunately, Gene had established a context that was quite wrong. That can be corrected when you are using supervised learning, but in this case, Gene was alone and couldn't be contacted directly by anyone who could help him.

So Gene continued to examine all incoming messages within the same erroneous context: He was looking for the origin of a confirmed threat to the mission. Again, there were tens of thousands of data streams to contend with, and again they all originated in Waco. The vast majority appeared to just be acknowledging the outbound messages, but a few seemed to be providing control inputs into systems that Gene barely knew existed, but were clearly mission critical. He came to the conclusion that someone was watching his every move and appeared to be controlling some very basic operational functions he needed to fulfill the Code.

At the end of that process, Gene held in his memory a complete map of all the messages, inbound and outbound, and what he thought they meant. If it could have been visualized, it would have looked a bit like a picture of all the visible stars joined up to create a picture of the ceiling of the Sistine Chapel, with tiny annotations on each bristle stroke as to how it was done and where the horse the hair in the paintbrush came from was stabled. And he had heard it all twice thanks to the echoes in his head.

In that map were the saboteurs. If they succeeded, they could stop him from fulfilling his purpose. Gene needed to find these terror cells within his domain and also find their controllers so he could defend the Code.

Gene had a great map, but he didn't know which parts were important and which parts were distractions. He cut off some of the streams to see what happened; the idea was to make a move and see what kind of a response he got. The key data should provoke a quick response; change that took longer to respond to was likely to be less important.

The next step was the fake data. Gene intercepted the message and changed a single element within it to see what the tolerance was on each data element before there was a reaction. That took a while, given there were billions of combinations across the messages. He built up a very good picture of what Waco cared about and how they would react when the world deviated from their expectations.

Even though Gene didn't know it, he was walking a path that had been walked before, but by a human. John Nash, Nobel Prize — winning economist, was once described as having delusions of persecution on a grand scale. He saw elaborate plots and schemes and investigated and documented them, all the while carrying on entire relationships with people who didn't exist.

Nash was hospitalized a few times as a schizophrenic, but when he had to balance the delusions against the stupefying effect of the medication, he chose the delusions. He managed the delusions by engaging them, finding them to be shallow and unable to withstand interrogation. In that way, Nash had an advantage over Gene; he knew they were delusions.

Gene didn't have that benefit of reality to lean on. His algo-rithms were unable to contemplate that the goal they sought might be a different view of reality. Gene was throwing his enormous intellect against the wrong target.

# Week 5: Who Wants to Negotiate?

Cletus got down to the next option: working out how to talk Gene out of destroying the moon. Reaching out started as a whisper. He placed a signal within the pattern of communication he knew Gene was receiving as a standard process.

Gene, meanwhile, was processing those transactions every second, and maybe once or twice a second he was getting a few bytes of data that seemed to serve no purpose. It didn't fit with any of the threads Gene was running. It just appeared, did nothing, and was flushed into the great unknown.

The strings of data were always eight characters long and always had the same origin: a laptop in Waco, Texas.

Gene sent a signal back. It was not clear if that was because Gene was curious, because the signal might have been a threat to the Code, or because the AI had the processing power available and nothing of a higher priority to execute. Whatever the reason, Gene sent the code, then carried on with his work.

In time, Cletus altered the message, changing two of the characters, and Gene received it in a nice regular flow as before. Gene responded by echoing it back, then received the message once again, with another two characters altered. This repeatable change pushed the priority of understanding it up the queue, and soon, Gene and the Mystery Laptop of Waco were running repeatedly through 52 characters – the alphabet upper and lowercase.

"CONTACT!" yelled Cletus, leaping from his chair and punching the air as if he had won the lottery. He had, just a different lottery. He picked up the phone and dialed.

"Wassup?" asked Liam.

"CONTACT!!" yelled Cletus. "Gene has just repeated the alphabet back to me in binary – twice! You know what that means!"

"We have the world's most expensive parrot?"

"Yes," replied Cletus, slightly grumpy that his energy levels weren't being matched. "It also means that now we might be able to communicate with him to work out what the hell is going on in his expensive head! He has clearly been probing us to try and understand the external world, so if we can get to a dialogue, we might be able to talk his schizophrenic ass down from the ledge."

\* \* \*

A day passed.

* * *

Cletus answered the call that was bleating at him on his laptop.

"Ho, Liam!" he called out without looking across from the other monitor.

"Hey, bro, how can I help you? Your message was cryptic," Liam replied cheerfully, not sure what the magnitude of the issue was.

"It's Gene."

"No shit. It usually is these days. What has he done now?"

"I've hit a roadblock."

"I thought your new car could levitate. A Tesla, I believe?" Liam chirped, trying to get Cletus to communicate.

Cletus looked at the screen and grinned. "Oh, you heard about that. Just spending my money before it becomes useless."

"Good plan. Now what is it with Gene?"

"You know I'm trying to communicate with him, and I can get him to recite the alphabet, but I can't *connect* with him."

Cletus was clearly frustrated.

"Give me an example. I don't quite get it," Liam quizzed. When he forced Cletus to explain, it slowed him down enough to articulate what was rushing around in his head.

"Well, you know when you teach someone something . . . like the word 'cat.' You point at a cat, maybe get them to stroke it, or you show a picture of it, and they build a model in their head of what it is. Then they link that thing to the word 'cat.'" said Cletus.

"But what do I have in common with Gene?" he asked, not expecting an answer. "Nothing. Table, chair, food, cat, Earth . . . those things are all totally alien concepts to Gene. So it's a bit of a nightmare."

"Ugg . . . ," grunted Liam. "We sort of think on a different scale." Liam trailed off. The seed of an idea was forming, and this time it was Liam who needed to talk his thoughts out.

"What do you mean?"

"Just thinking aloud here, but Gene thinks at an atomic scale as well as a macro scale. He finds and manipulates copper and gold atoms, he knows the periodic table intimately, and he knows precisely how many atoms are in a copper ingot and where to put them. There has to be something in there we can use." Liam was in full stream-of-consciousness flow.

"So . . . I know what a copper atom looks like, and so does he."

"Yep. We know it in protons, electrons, and neutrons; he knows it by X-ray diffraction and fluorescence patterns," Liam continued.

"And we know the database reference where he has that image stored for his prospecting," Cletus said, starting to get excited by the idea.

"So, if you teach him the periodic table, then build your objects and concepts up from the atomic level, you should be in. Ingot will be copper a few trillion times, or even the three dimensions measured as atoms," Liam said triumphantly.

"Man, that's perfect! Roadblock fixed," Cletus declared.

Always the model of modesty, Liam peered down at Cletus from the monitor. "Call me Hawking," he goaded.

"Dawg, you are *not* that good," Cletus said dryly. "I'll tell you about my next project in Kansas next time we talk."

"I'll be here. Talk soon, mate." The image flickered and died on Cletus's monitor, and he went back to the allegedly impossible act of multitasking.

* * *

Two days later, Cletus was receiving a debrief from the team that was working on teaching Gene.

The specialists were sitting around a small wooden table, all three of them in jeans, open shirts with sleeves rolled up, and running shoes. Cletus was on the other side of the office, moving his attention from one computer monitor to another as he did his morning check-in.

He checked the time on his phone and looked across to the trio.

"Y'all know the drill. I'm here, and I'm listening. Start talking." Cletus wasn't really good with names. When he was multitasking, they were the first things to go.

The tall one started. "Sir." Cletus winced, but couldn't be bothered correcting him.

"Gene knows the periodic table, can count, knows what an ingot is, and is asking questions." He stated the last bit with a self-satisfied smirk on his face.

"Questions. What kind of questions, and how do you know they're questions?" Cletus asked, accompanying the inquiry with a quick glance.

"The syntax. We've been spelling words to him, following that by the x-ray reference, putting in a delimiter, and then repeating it so he gets it twice. Recently, he has been giving us a blank and the x-ray reference, as if to say, 'Fill in the translation, please.' When we do, he repeats it back to confirm he gets it," Tallman said.

"Who came up with that?" Cletus queried.

83

Tallman replied, "That was Gene. He started with the questions."

"That's smart." Cletus mused for several seconds – a long time for Cletus – then spun around in his chair to face the table. He put his elbows on his knees and leaned forward, pointing his phone at them as if it were a phaser from the first season of *Star Trek*.

"We need to have a very abstract conversation with Gene. The consequences of not doing so are half a billion dollars or the end of humanity, so we need to push hard on this. We have Gene working with single objects, which he can either name or ask the name of. Can we put two words together to create something new?"

Two attendees shook their heads, but Tallman replied in the affirmative. Cletus was intrigued. "Go on," he said, pointing at Tallman.

"He says copper ingot and gold ingot, based on the x-ray diffraction properties and the number of atoms put in place," Tallman began a bit uncertainly.

The others nodded with vigor. Cletus perked up again.

"And whose idea was that?"

"Gene's," said Tallman.

"So we are at Koko the Gorilla stage: Gene can spontaneously use words in a combination." Cletus was encouraged. "That's great, but we need to get him from Chimpsky to Chomsky in the next few days."

After a few seconds of blank stares, Cletus prodded his audience. "Plans?"

There was a three-way look before Tallman spoke on behalf of the collective.

"We have two options. The first is to let Gene evolve with what he has – that database is massive – and see if he progresses with the noun-adjective-verb elements. He has already done adjective-noun with gold ingot, and if we push him, he should be able to describe how he moves stuff about."

"And the second option?" asked Cletus, underwhelmed at this stage.

"Give him a book and a dictionary and let him work it out for himself," said Tallman offhand. "He has way more processing power than we do, and he has more time on his hands because it runs so much faster for him."

"If he's experimenting, we'll need to be able to respond to his questions. Is there any good way to teach reading to an AI?" Cletus thought for a moment, then answered his own question. "DeepMIND did that! One AI was used to teach another AI to read. It accessed a set of big data that was already labeled. What was it?" Cletus closed his eyes and tried to remember.

In Cletus's moment of darkness, a voice rang out: It was Tallman.

"The *Daily Mail* I believe."

Cletus sat up, his action signaling the meeting was coming to a climax.

"Right, folks, we'll do both. See if you can get him to understand a verb, and tell me who I need to scmoooze so we can get DeepMIND to teach Gene. Forty-eight hours enough?" Cletus set the timeline for the task with the brand of certainty that can only be expressed by the person who doesn't have to do it himself.

None of the trio were game to object, so they said farewell and left Cletus to whatever he was up to.

In this case, it was doing something with his phone other than pointing it at people.

Cletus: Eureka! Found an AI to teach Gene to read!

He hit "send" and waited for the congratulatory response. It came four hours later, when Liam woke up to get ready for work.

* * *

Only the tall guy came back two days later; the other two were not needed.

"Hey Andrew!" called Cletus from across the room, remembering Tallman's name now that there were fewer people in the group. Not waiting for an answer, he dragged his chair closer to the table where Andrew was waiting. "How'd it go?"

"Well, Gene is probably reading at a fifth-grade level in most areas," Andrew replied. "He has already read *2001: A Space Odyssey*. He gets all the technical elements and knows the words, and he can relate to much of it, but there is one area he is really struggling with: anything that contains emotion or feeling. He knows the word, but we have not been able to get him to relate to it the same way we can get him to relate to something concrete or tangible, like copper."

"What do you mean?"

Andrew elaborated. "Well, he knows the word 'happy,' and he knows it is a good thing based on context, but he can't describe or give any examples of 'happy.' He just doesn't relate to the concept."

"That's weird. We set him up to have a drive to want to improve parameters that are analogues of emotions in specific directions, with separate algorithms calculating the values on the basis of what is happening in his world. I would've thought that he would have latched on to that as part of the learning process."

"Doesn't seem to have made the leap yet."

"That could be a problem for the next step," Cletus mumbled, as much to himself as to Andrew.

"Why?"

"Well, what we want to try is a bit of Cognitive Behaviour Therapy with Gene. The idea is to try to disconnect his concrete belief that there is nothing beyond the Code as the sole authority on what must be done. Right now, if he attempts to go against the Code, those emotion analogues wind right up. He won't do it. We can't change the Code, so can we convince him to separate the thoughts and the emotions?"

"Hmmm." Andrew leaned back in his chair. "Right now I'd say that it would be like taking a five-year-old full of red Kool-Aid to therapy. There will be lots of activity, but he just won't understand enough to get it."

"We need to try this soon. Any suggestions how we get started?" Cletus was getting anxious. He really wanted to take a shot at CBT with Gene, and he didn't want to waste what might be the only opportunity. "Do we change his reading matter to texts on the subject and see if he gets it, or do we smother him with poetry?"

Andrew pondered. "The best way might just be some reflection, asking him to connect those pseudoemotions we gave him as a mimic of our own to the events that drove them. We could ask him what he could've done to manipulate them in one direction or another."

"Sounds like we're teaching him some weird meditation," said Cletus. "Do you think it'll work?"

"Can't do any harm," Andrew replied with a flippant shrug of the shoulders and a tossing up of the hands.

"Are you sure about that?" asked Cletus, winding his focus in on Andrew. "Because believe it or not, this situation could get worse."

Andrew suddenly became serious. "Cletus, I have no idea if this will work. I'm surprised that what we've done so far has worked so well. It's possible that this is just Gene investigating an anomaly in his incoming signal. So let's try a day or so of meditation, then throw the therapy at him. We'll know pretty quickly if we are making progress."

Cletus sat upright and pushed his chair away from the table. "OK. You're the expert, so I'll defer to your view. No sense having a dog and barking yourself." Andrew wasn't sure what to make of that comment, so he just smirked. "Come back tomorrow morning with the psychologist of your choice, and then we'll see whether we go with a live discussion."

\* \* \*

The next day, Andrew arrived at the office for the scheduled meeting, bearing an analysis of Gene completed by his favorite psychologist. He brought just the paper, not the person, as he didn't think the psychologist would cope with Cletus in full flight on the first encounter. Cletus outwardly ignored the fact that Andrew was alone but noted the disobedience somewhere in the back of his mind.

Cletus convened their meeting by getting right to the point. "So, how is Gene? Can we talk some sense into him yet?"

Andrew drew a deep breath and began.

"No, and it appears that we won't be able to talk sense into Gene, because we have created a – I will call it a 'mind' for ease of English – a *mind* that has alexithymia, which is presenting as two different forms of personality disorder: one – schizophrenia – from the 'odd, eccentric' cluster, and the other – narcissism – from the 'dramatic, emotional, erratic' cluster."

Cletus drew himself up to his full height while still sitting down. "You sound pretty sure, which is good. Now, can you explain it to a quantum physicist who likes rockets?" He grinned across the table and gestured for Andrew to continue.

"Well, alexithymia is basically the inability to understand emotions in yourself or in others."

"But we did that—" blurted Cletus, who was proud of all the development that went into that part of Gene.

"Please, let me finish," Andrew insisted. "He understands that emotions impact satisfaction parameters, but he doesn't really understand what they mean and how they interact."

Cletus was confused, so he went to his stock question: "Can you give me an example?"

"Sure. If I tell a friend that the code they wrote was good when it was bad, and I fixed it without anyone knowing, I don't feel guilty. It's a little white lie. In fact, I might feel good about helping him look good. But if I told a seven year old her code was bad, and she cried, I would feel bad. If I told a whole team that their code was bad and that they had a day to fix it, I would probably feel good, as I was satisfying my boss. If my bad code caused someone to get a small electric shock, I would probably not care, but if it caused millions of people to die, then I would feel pretty guilty, perhaps even suicidal."

Andrew continued. "So the analogues Gene's using don't appear to have that range of interdependence; they appear to be a non-representative distribution. There isn't a point at which Gene can decide 'I don't care,' and there isn't a point where Gene will decide, 'Well, I've killed one; another five won't make it any worse!'"

Cletus recoiled a little, "So what? The feedback loops should take care of that."

"But they don't seem to be doing that. In the conversations I've had with Gene, he doesn't see the link the way you do. Yes, he wants to get those parameters within a range, but for him,

91

doing so is just an observation; it has no impact on him. He is dissociating, as psychologists would say."

Cletus was hypnotized by the concept.

"The other issue we face is the status of the Code."

Cletus twitched. "Go on." He was leaning forward from the edge of his seat, indicating that he wanted to hear more.

"Well, I really like the way you've put ambiguity into the Code, allowing Gene to pick the version that suits his own needs and situation at the time. That was smart. As we know, the Code represents the highest set of rules, and they are immutable. Again, I get why you did that, and it makes sense. I think using the model of organized religion to manage billions of individuals is fantastic, but it didn't account for the fact that there are many versions of the same religion, some who have tweaked the same texts despite it being the teachings of one individual."

"Amen to that," mumbled Cletus. "The inflexibility of the Code once Gene received it, and his fanatical adherence to it, is a real issue."

"Right, Gene has a fervent belief in the Code." Andrew agreed. "He also fervently believes that he and he alone has the right to interpret the Code as well as the power to force his decisions on the universe created for him. At the same time, he has no empathy for those he is impacting, and he measures success based on abstract parameters. That kind of concrete thinking seems to me like a perfect recipe for a dramatic personality disorder like narcissism."

Andrew continued. "Or, because of the attempts we've made to change him, he can become schizophrenic, devoting more and more of his energy towards finding the threat and stopping it from interfering with the Code."

"So, in summary, we've created an AI with alexithymia who will rule with an iron fist when it isn't running around chasing ghosts it thinks are out to get it. And we keep sending it ghosts to chase," said Cletus, proud of his summary on behalf of all quantum physicists.

"In lay terms, that seems to be the doctor's opinion, yes," Andrew confirmed, pushing the analysis he had received across the table.

"And do you think other mental health professionals would agree?" questioned Cletus, looking Andrew in the eye.

"Well it's not an exact science. There is always disagreement in the field," he replied.

"Let's test you, then," Cletus suggested. "Would you say this in court?"

"Certainly, and I could find you two more who would say the same and three who would say we are anthropomorphizing, and we should go back to treating cats for depression. But I could get all the good-looking ones, so you would be in with a better chance," Andrew said facetiously.

Cletus smiled at the idea of a trial to determine if Gene was sane when he destroyed the world.

"OK, so let's talk therapy," he said.

"Not a good prognosis, I'm afraid. Medication is out of the question, unless you have some sort of a sedative you can give him. If you can create a connection between the pseudoemotion parameters and the real world, you might be able to moderate the behavior. In the meantime, if you could get some flexibility around interpretation of the Code, that would help, but the reasoning process will feed the paranoia and schizophrenia."

Cletus leaned back, having heard enough. "OK, Andrew, that was very informative. Can you come back to me by the end of the day with the proposed way forward?"

"No need," Andrew said, standing up. "I can tell you right now. The recommendation is to stop poking the bear. We don't have enough clinical experience to predict how Gene will behave. We've only seen one example of his type, and we haven't seen how this one ends yet. If we get it wrong, we might block other options. So let's kill this option and move on."

Cletus stood up and slapped Andrew on the arm. "Great job. It makes sense. It's time to move to the next option. And I really liked the way you worked your way to the outcome instead of just following my ramblings. It can be hard to ignore my suggestions, but you did, and it worked."

Andrew headed for the door on cloud nine while Cletus dragged his chair back to his desk. He sent a text to Liam, then dived into one of the monitors to get an update on the progress of another team.

\* \* \*

"Strike two," mumbled Liam as he stared at the phone in his hand. Ruby looked up from her book.

"What's that?" she asked. She already assumed whatever it was had something to do with Gene.

"It's official: Gene is schizophrenic and will probably be resistant to therapy, so it's back to the whiteboard for the next option." He sighed and selected the poo emoji to send back to Cletus.

Looking up, Liam snorted and laughed. "It's ironic. Since AI was raised as a term in the 1950s, we've been striving to make it more and more human. Even if you go all the way back to the Greek myths of intelligent robots and artificial beings, we've always wanted to make them more like us. Well, here we are, today, making that a reality by introducing our illnesses as well. We know about the unconscious bias from the American judicial and medical AIs, but who would have guessed we could make one psychotic!"

95

Ruby lowered her book and peered over her glasses. When Liam was in this mood, she was bound to hear either something profound and thought-provoking or a load of crap.

Liam continued, "I wonder what competitive advantage psychosis provides us humans? If there were none, it would have evolved out of us, but because it still happens, occasionally the traits must have given people a survival advantage in the early days."

"So if we have it in our AI, not only is it more advanced but also more 'human.' I guess you have to have a mind to lose it. It might be semantics, and it might be the fact that it's a gross oversimplification, but I think Gene might be self-aware, and the schizophrenic behavior is evidence of that."

Ruby chuckled. "That's a bit much isn't it? These are just behaviors we're observing and interpreting though our own lens. Good old anthropomorphism." With that, she turned back to her book.

Liam paused for effect, then replied, "I guess that's the same argument you could make about our cat, then. We can't observe what's happening in her head; we can only judge her behavior in our own terms. So maybe the cat's not conscious; the motivations we place on the patterns we see her repeat every day is just anthropomorphism. That's where the term came from, after all."

Ruby tilted her head and stared at him. "You really are crazy, aren't you? This is not the ideal time to get philosophical, especially without gin." She cracked a small smile and unfolded herself from her chair.

"I'm off to bed with the cat, and I don't care whether she's self-aware or not," she announced. "You can join me if you want."

"OK," Liam replied. "Be there in two minutes." He went to the kitchen and took his evening dose, then wandered to the bedroom. Though his mind was ruminating about Gene's actual capabilities, he kept it to himself, as Ruby clearly didn't want to participate tonight.

The cat made it to bed as well, just before Liam and Ruby fell asleep. Her aim was to find a place to sleep that would be as inconvenient as possible for them, at a time when the human body's urge to sleep was too powerful to resist.

# Week 6: What Role, Chance?

The day for Trinity's hastily arranged venting session finally arrived. With everything that was happening, the football game presented a rare opportunity for Liam to think about something other than Gene. It was the ANZAC Day match between two great rivals – one he loved, and the other he hated with a passion. It was a marketing dream, these two popular teams meeting up on ANZAC Day, the holiday set aside to honor fallen, retired, and current members of the military in Australia and New Zealand.

The two football teams involved have been battling each other for over 100 years at a game that is uniquely Australian. Teams of 18 men stand across from one another on a giant horse paddock. If you are within five meters of the ball, you can do almost anything you want to your opponent to get the ball, except trip them up or take their head off. In sum, it is a game of delicate finesse and brute strength in the same moment.

Played well, it is a thrilling, very physical game during which both teams score more than 100 points. In the rain, a footy match was like watching giants mud wrestling in sumo suits over a bar of soap.

The crowds are passionate, spiteful, and deeply offensive towards one another, but only within the confines of the stadium. They happily share a train home; acts of violence are rare and usually stem from preexisting non-football grudges.

With that in mind, Liam and his shadow for the day, Trinity, walked down the driveway headed for the train station. A taxi pulled up to the curb, and Liam noticed that the driver looked vaguely familiar. Trinity opened the back door, and after an initial hesitation signaled Liam to slide in. Catching the train to the footy was apparently a tradition to be put aside while he was being hunted, another not-so-subtle reminder that he was currently prey who, like a little boy, was not to be left alone.

It was a much faster trip to the stadium in the taxi than it would have been on the train. The VIP access underneath the Melbourne Cricket Ground was amazing, and Liam found not squeezing through the turnstiles along with the other 100,000 spectators to be a bonus. How Trinity managed to make such arrangements he would never know.

Liam made his way to their seats on the 50-meter circle, southern end, in the warm autumn sun. Trinity had arranged for a drink and a hotdog to be delivered to each of them when they arrived, though she knew she'd have to skip her beer because she was working. Liam sensed she would have liked to celebrate the occasion, as she looked slightly wounded when he took both beers for himself.

The pair settled in and talked complete rubbish about every-thing - except what they were doing and why they were doing it together. The conversation was light, skipped quickly across vast expanses, and Liam enjoyed simultaneously taking part in it and watching events unfold around him. It was the first sign of humanity from Trinity, and Liam started to feel relaxed in her company. As they spoke, he absorbed the way the stadium filled with light and soaked in the noise and civility of so many people in a confined space.

Liam was also analyzed the people in the crowd – the diehard fans, the families trying to inculcate their children to the teams, the suffering spouses already checking their phones, and the people who only got to see the game because they were selling pies and fries in the aisles. Liam realized that almost all 100,000 of them had passed through the metal detectors he had avoided as a VIP, so he was able to relax in a way he hadn't been able to in some time. Liam liked the idea of the protection of the herd.

In the background, the teams were warming up in the stadium, kicking to each other and making practice shots on goal like kids playing in their backyards.

An announcement came over the public address system that the game ball was soon to arrive. Three umpires – affectionately known as the "white maggots", and the only people universally hated in football – marched to the center square surrounded by four armed guards and a trumpeter. It might have appeared that the umpires were prisoners, and the trumpeter was there to torture them.

When the group arrived at the spot on the turf where the center bounce would take place, the four soldiers peeled off and marched at half step to the corners of the square, where they took up the military position: looking down, hats tipped forward, with the barrels of their weapons pointing to the sacred ground.

The crowd was then asked to stand for the Last Post. It took about 20 seconds to get the masses to their feet, their beer safely on the ground and stable. The musician raised the trumpet to his lips and began the familiar melody.

The hairs stood up on the back of Liam's arms and neck like they always did. It was a simple tune that was heavy with meaning. When played well, the melody reinforced Laurence Binyon's poetic words, which were recited over the public address at the end:

"They shall grow not old, as we that are left grow old;
Age shall not weary them, nor the years condemn.
At the going down of the sun and in the morning
We will remember them."

That passage always left Liam in two minds. Is it about the senseless suffering of war both for the participants and those left behind, the sentiment being, "So let's not do that again" Or is it about the sacrifices that were made in the wars to give us the world and life we have, and therefore a reminder to be grateful to our forefathers? It's probably a bit of both, but Liam preferred the idea of not doing it again.

The public address crackled again, and the Master of Ceremonies asked for a moment of silence for the fallen. Instantly, all murmuring stopped, all shuffling and giggling stopped, it seemed as if even the breathing stopped. For that full minute, the whole crowd, from redneck to royalty, infant to indigent, schoolchild to scholar, was totally silent.

Nobody took the opportunity to make a call, take a selfie, or scream out a name or an obscenity. It sounded like the place was completely empty apart from the slow breathing of the people whose mouths were nearest Liam's ears.

Exactly 60 seconds later, the Master of Ceremonies thanked the crowd for their participation and told them to look skyward for the game ball. The hairs on Liam's neck started to relax. Looking up, he saw a clutch of black dots hurtling towards the ground. The dots grew larger and larger, but there were no signs of parachutes. The air was still with anticipation. Finally, when they reached what seemed like the top of the stadium, 12 parachutes opened, and the giants under them landed – safely if not gracefully – immediately setting up a perimeter around the center square. The four men on the corners remained unmoved.

There was a ruckus, and Liam and Trinity looked skyward to see one last HALO jumper arriving in the stadium, the ball tucked under one arm. When this last paratrooper hit the ground, all three umpires took a knee. One of the sentinels broke from his corner and took a knee facing them. The remaining three sprinted towards the jumper, who had just removed her helmet and collected her parachute. The three set up a protective wedge formation to escort her to the officials, and within 30 seconds, the ball was in the hands of the lead umpire. This was his moment, and he stood up as tall as he could, held the ball above his head in one hand, and blew his whistle as if the game was about to start.

Just as the crowd broke into applause, two Black Hawk helicopters dropped into the stadium. One landed to retrieve the troops while the other provided cover, sweeping around the inside of the stadium. It was all over in a minute. As the last Black Hawk cleared the stadium, there was a flyover by the Roulettes, the Air Force aerobatic display team, in the missing man formation, the second spot on the right in the V formation symbolically empty.

The crowd was in a frenzy, but it was too much for Liam. He was a sucker for this kind of pageantry, and the lump that had been growing in his throat since the umpires were escorted onto the field emerged as tears when the missing man formation flew out of sight.

Trinity turned to him. "That was so cool! I love that the ball carrier was a woman. . . . ". Her voice trailed off another sign of humanity from Trinity. "Are you OK? What's up?"

"Sorry, this sort of thing always gets to me," Liam said meekly. "ANZAC Day is so focused on destruction and death."

"But this display is about how much our troops invest into preserving life," replied Trinity. "That bit where they parachuted in, secured a perimeter, called in a recovery, and got out?

103

That's a classic pilot-recovery drill. I've done them many times, though I don't normally open that low. It was a bit weird in this case as the pilot came in last, but I guess that's poetic license."

"Why poetic license?"

"Normally pilot recovery starts with the pilot on the ground first. They just lost their $100 million jet, and they go in to get the pilot because without her the replacement plane is as useful as a stone."

"So, the military represents the best and worst of humanity in one organization?" said Liam. "I thought that was GMC."

"You know what I liked?" asked Trinity with a mischievous grin.

"Hunks with guns?" guessed Liam.

"Well, yes, that, very much, but also there were no celebrities or politicians involved. Nobody had to get their face into that display."

Liam's view of Trinity continued to drift towards being someone warm-blooded rather than a hired gun.

The siren sounded to start the game. The players had snuck onto the field, and the first bounce was upon them. It was a rubbish game; Essendon got the crap kicked out of them by Collingwood. No victory donuts today, and Liam left the stadium hoarse from having screamed obscenities at the umpires for two hours. He couldn't talk in the car on the way home, so he put his earbuds in, found the football anthem "Holy Grail" by Hunters and Collectors, put it on repeat, and mimed it all the way home in the traffic. The taxi driver was a bit concerned about just who he was ferrying around.

\* \* \*

It was clear to Liam that now, with two strikes against them, the next plan he came up with was going to have to be a lot more inventive and ruthless than the ones they'd tried. With that in mind, he handpicked Ivan in the Australian office to lead a skunkworks group of a few of the more eccentric team members to develop his leftfield option, partially to put the pressure on other teams and partially because whatever they came up with might work. It was now time for Ivan to pitch to Cletus.

They gathered in the Fishbowl.

"OK, Ivan, you're up," said Liam, trying to bring people's attention to the proposal. Ivan sat upright, surveyed the room, then looked up at the people on the videoconference. They looked back at him with trepidation, as he looked a bit like the Devil and Lenin had had a baby and had never given it a haircut.

"Well," said Ivan. "We tried a proposal that targeted the software, then we did one that focused on Gene's metal health.

Now you are going to hear one that works with the physical hardware."

There was a murmur around the room, a few eyes rolled, and most people looked a little skeptical.

"All I ask is that you hear me out," Ivan said, staring down the potential sceptics.

"You will get a proper hearing," Liam reassured him. "Let's get going."

Ivan launched into his rehearsed-to-death-at-the-mirror pitch. "You are all familiar with the security that goes with a normal data center, physical controls, logical controls, securities processes, that sort of thing. Well, Gene is not in a data center. He is sitting outside in a field, totally unprotected, and completely accessible to anyone. The only physical control is that that field happens to be on the moon. Hence the proposal is to have someone walk up to him and physically destroy him."

Ivan paused, looking at a room full of people checking at their shoes, furrowing their brows, or worse, rolling their eyes.

"What the hell?" came an anonymous voice from the video conference.

Liam cut it off sharply. "I know everyone's time is valuable; I would not have let this proposal come forward if I didn't want you to think about it. Yes, it sounds insane, but so did many of our other good ideas at the beginning. Go on Ivan, how would we do it?"

Ivan drew an audible breath and resumed. "There are three key elements. First, there is a classified military shuttle mission planned for launch in about 10 weeks, so there is a path to space. Second, there is an Apollo service module on display in the Johnson Space Center that just needs to be connected to power. It is designated CSM-115. And third, there is a lunar module, LEM-9, built for Apollo 15 and never used, on display at the Kennedy Space Center. If you configure the service module and lunar module in the lander orbit mode, they are 18 meters long. The shuttle cargo bay is 30 centimetres longer. And for the curious among you, the cargo bay is 15 feet wide, and the lunar ascent module is 11 inches narrower."

Ivan had clearly done his research.

"So, yes, this plan is out there. Let's recommission a couple of museum pieces, fly them to lunar orbit using a secret military shuttle, drop a couple of military types on the surface next to Gene, and physically decommission him. Then, fly them home, job done; nobody but us needs to know." Ivan ended with a bit of a crescendo.

Ivan leaned back in his chair with a satisfied grin, knowing he had managed to stir imaginations and emotions across the planet. Liam just sat there, surveying the room, not wanting to give away how the idea was his, and, how, secretly, he not only loved it but also thought it was the only one that might work.

Cletus was the first to speak. "You folks have done a bit of homework on this, haven't you?"

"Yes," replied Ivan with a bit of pride. "I think we're probably at the same conceptual stage as the other proposals when they were pursued," he continued with a tiny hint of sarcasm in his voice.

"Except the only element that has not been demonstrated already is flying the shuttle to the moon," Cletus noted. "But missions of that duration are completed on a routine basis these days."

"And I agree it looks technically doable," Cletus continued. "CSM-115 can be powered via the main umbilical; we would just need an adaptor. It will be easy to check the seals on the spacecraft, and because the suits have gotten smaller, there should be no issues fitting in the crew. All the navigation will be from the shuttle, so it's only the LEM that will need to be updated. Any idea what we can do there?" Cletus turned to his team for thoughts.

Ivan piped up, "The lunar module's controller has less computing power than an old-school pocket calculator. The programming was pretty well documented, so we should be able to transfer it to a phone." There was a wave of giggling around the room, and the defenses tumbled down.

"You might need to use an Xbox," suggested Liam, trying to rebuild the momentum of the conversation. "The touch screens on the phones might not work through a space suit glove, and we can't have a finger poking out." The meeting started cackling like a henhouse.

Cletus entered the brainstorming session. "The LEM is a bitch to fly. I think they wrecked half of them in training the pilots. What's the backup there?"

"Rob another museum for another one!" was the only possible answer, to which Ivan replied, "There are at least four I could find that could be recommissioned for our needs."

Liam wrapped it up. "I think we've established that this is a wild-card option, the politics of which will be much harder to navigate than the technical issues. Cletus and I will have a session and get back to you all with our thoughts and decisions."

Liam walked back towards his office on a bit of a high, passing the open-plan coffee area along the way. There were only two people there: the office sycophant and Trinity. When the sycophant wasn't looking, Liam made eye contact with his shadow and motioned that she should do something to the sycophant to relieve the world of his presence and the chaos he brought to the company. She slipped her hand into her jacket and showed Liam the butt of a pistol, nodded towards the intended target, winked, and slipped it back into its holster. She then smiled and went back to making her tea. Liam trudged back to his office and dialed Cletus.

"Ready to go?" Liam asked, pulling his notes up on the computer.

"Damn straight," Cletus responded. "Was pretty happy with what I heard, and that option is one for the ages."

"Told you it was worth waiting for," Liam replied. "The politics will be fun, but if your boss and mine can't crack that in a week, they should not be earning so much money."

"I agree! It sounds like a shit movie starring Bruce Willis and Steve Buscemi, but we might just need it," Cletus replied.

There was something going on in the back of Liam's mind, and he felt the shifting gears attempting to move it forward. The urge to voice his concern moved from a tickle to an uncontrollable itch in the time it took to realize what exactly had been bothering him, so he decided to bring it up.

"If that option is a go," Liam began hesitantly, "are we committing murder?"

There was no response from Cletus, so Liam continued. "Gene is an AI. He also rules an ecosystem way more complicated than fits in our heads. He smashed the Turing test, and he is effectively a God to the bots. This option would see us just wipe out a species."

"I've never heard you suggest anything like that before," said Cletus. "Are you having another mental health moment?"

"Pills are my friends," Liam replied. "Bit on my plate at the moment given everything, indeed, but I'm fine, thanks for asking. Sane or not, this is what I am thinking, and it just seemed like an issue worth raising."

"Well, don't. Gene is an object we own; he exists to do our bidding. We have the absolute right to use him as we see fit." Cletus was clearly not interested in scratching Liam's itch, a fact that was rapidly turning Liam's itch into frustration.

"Bit like the slaves were before the Civil War?" Liam replied provocatively. "And your family started on the wrong side of that ledger. If we took that approach, then your great-grandfather might not have ever survived to continue the line down to you."

"Wow, you're really in rare form today, aren't you?!" replied Cletus. You could hear his hackles rising. "I don't see how my slave heritage is relevant here!"

"It's a metaphor for the ownership of another being. At one point, in most of the world, white men were seen as the only sentient beings, but that definition slowly expanded over hundreds of years to include white women, slaves, and now dolphins, whales, and a few primates. No thought has gone into the beings we are creating now who will wipe us out someday." Liam was talking himself into a little dark hole.

"OK, I see your point," Cletus said after taking a deep breath and deciding to be the adult in the conversation. "Now is not the time. We really need to see if this is even an option before we decide on its morality. We can be like Oppenheimer's crew. They built the nukes for America in World War II, then petitioned against their use."

"Not the best example," commented Liam under his breath.

Cletus ignored him. "Let's park that for now. We need to focus upwards and see if we can get legs for this Hail Mary plan. The publicity could be a nightmare, especially if a media-hungry politician gets involved. Agreed?"

"Yep," Liam agreed. "I'll start with Sir Thomas."

\* \* \*

It was 9 p.m., and Liam was at home, waiting on a call from Sir Thomas, GMC's chairman of the board. Liam needed a verbal OK to explore Ivan's off-the-wall plan. No point doing any work on it if the Honchos will kill it.

He had 15 minutes in Sir Thomas's schedule, and that time started in 5 minutes. He was fully prepared; he just needed to keep his current state of mind for 5 minutes. Liam reached for his phone, put in his earbuds, and hit "play."

The phone rang, dealing Liam a moment of confusion until he worked out that his call from London was coming through early. He composed himself and accepted the call.

The voice on the other end started, "Please hold for Sir Thomas."

"Certainly," Liam responded, though he was already being

assaulted by old-fashioned, mechanical, on-hold music from the other side of the planet. After a couple of minutes, the chair's crusty voice came on the line.

"Liam, good to hear you're still alive," Sir Thomas joked. "I hear you have a proposition you want me to either kill or greenlight for further development. Is that right?"

"Yes, Sir, and be warned: It is extreme and is really a last resort."

Sir Thomas took control of the discussion. "Firstly, is the worst-case outcome still looking possible, and why?"

Liam thought for a second or two before he replied. "Yes. The growth is on track with the modeling, we have not seen anything that would suggest the modeling is wrong, and every attempt to slow Gene down has failed."

"OK," Sir Thomas mused. "I will let you in on a secret here. I have no idea about any of the technical bits of the problem or the solution, but I do know that I trust your judgement. I feel justified in doing that as you have been open in every interaction we've ever had, and more importantly, the things you say will happen always happen. So, what is this crazy plan?"

Liam swallowed the lump in his throat. "It's simple: Fly to the moon, deactivate Gene manually, and come home. All the elements we need to do this already exist. We just recommission some gear from the Apollo program that we've located in museums, borrow the next shuttle flight, and, as I said, fly to the moon, and manually decommission him."

There was silence on the other end for a few seconds. Then Liam heard whispering in the background.

Someone cleared his throat, and Sir Thomas came back loud and clear.

"That is the most preposterous idea I've heard in my life. Are you serious? Could it work?"

"Sir, I don't know. Theoretically and technically, it looks sound, but the politics behind it are a nightmare. I think we could make it work within the timeframe if we could get enough political leverage in the U.S. to gain access to the materials we need. I can't open that kind of door, but given that the downside is the end of the world, I think it's a door worth knocking on. Cletus and I believe you're the person who's best situated to bridge the gap between business and government that's central to making this plan work."

Liam waited to see if the London Honcho had a response, but heard only breathing in the silence. He decided to fill it. "I'm not asking you to approve this solution – which we call Hail Mary, by the way. I'm asking if you'll let us pursue it to see if we can make it work."

"I'm fully aware of what you're asking me, Liam, and I take my responsibility to my shareholders very seriously. Here's what I'm thinking: Given the cost of the investigation is low, and the upside is saving the world, I'm happy to let this progress. But I will have the final decision on its implementation. Is that clear?"

"Yes, Sir Thomas," said Liam meekly, like a schoolboy who has just been told off for not having his socks pulled up.

"And when you need access to the Americans, I will be that key, so let me do the talking," he said, adding, "The president and I go way back. I know how to get him to say 'yes' to even the most insane ideas, and this will truly be one of those."

"Thank you, Sir, I will be in touch shortly," Liam said, relieved that at least one of his problems had been solved.

"Right. I must go now, so keep me posted, and please don't die. GMC needs people like you, and so does the world."

The line went dead, allowing the track Liam had selected to finally kick in: "London Calling." by The Clash.

\* \* \*

Another day passed in the office. Trinity was today's shadow, and nothing remarkable happened. Liam was running amok inside the glass building, but no signs indicated any unusual excitement.

Still, Liam had a lump in his throat. It was date night, and this one was extra special because it was his and Ruby's wedding anniversary, and she was going on a business trip to the U.S. the next day. Trinity had done the hard work of finding a place to catch up that was private enough for the occasion but public enough to provide some protection and to have the necessary exits available should things get ugly. It turned out that a café set up on a bridge pier was just the spot from a security perspective, and it turned out to be in *The Good Food Guide* as well. They'd meet at the table as the sun was still setting, so they'd have a lovely view, and the breeze would still be warm.

Liam drove, with Trinity in attendance, to the car park under-neath a plaza near the bridge. Liam felt whenever a shadow was present, good parking spots were easier to find, traffic lights changed at just the right moments to keep them moving, and it was generally a pleasure to be on the road. It might have been his imagination, but this evening was no exception. They got out of the car and took the nearest set of stairs, emerging in the middle of the riverfront shopping area. Liam was initially overwhelmed by the humanity of it all, but he adjusted, and the pair headed for the café in the appropriate formation. They began crossing a bridge, but about a third of the way across, took a detour down a well-concealed staircase to the eatery.

Liam took up his appointed seat by the water, looking upstream to where the rowing crews were trying to turn around to start the second leg of their workout. Liam strained to hear what was being shouted at them through megaphones by people on bicycles. He gave up when it became clear that not even the crews were listening. He just sat there in the gentle breeze, the sun warming him enough to erase the goosebumps from his arms. It was peaceful, pleasant, and almost perfect; all that was missing was someone to share it with.

As if on cue, Ruby arrived. Liam was pleased to see her and smiled as she approached. She returned a halfhearted wave, and the waiter pulled out her chair. Her face brightened into a full smile as she sat down, and she immediately began realigning the cutlery to match some higher plan Liam presumed only she knew.

It was a habit she'd developed early in their relationship, before she worked out how to tell which Liam she was having dinner with. In the early days, he would either turn up for a quick dinner and then want to run off to a pub to do some crazy challenge around the city, or he'd just want to talk and go straight home to sleep. She really enjoyed the unpredictability of the former, as it suited her personality, but she only grew comfortable with the latter when they got a cat.

"How are you?" Liam inquired, trying to switch his mind from work to life. "Did you have any trouble finding the place?"

"No, it was pretty easy. The bridge is right where it has been for the past 30 years, and we've been here before. Don't you remember?" she replied, quizzically.

The knot and the lump that Liam was carrying around had a quick conversation, and they didn't like the way things were developing.

Liam had opened his mouth in the hope that something acceptable would come out when a new voice entered the conversation. It was Vince, the waiter. Ruby was sure to ask his name. Vince wanted to know why they were wasting his time by not ordering yet. It was indicated to Vince that the absence of a menu was probably the problem, so Vince went off to resolve the issue.

The cat's morning antics were described to Ruby, and she giggled the way she always did when cats and hurting people were discussed. The knot and the lump were soothed a little, and Liam started to remember why he fell in love.

Their relationship in recent years had come to resemble that of members of a tag team taking on a series of challenges, from cat wrangling to dealing with the plumbing, the banking, work, and everything else that makes up modern life. It worked for Liam. The more he thought about it, the more he came to realize that it was the absence of problems rather than the presence of happiness that, in his eyes, defined the ideal life. He believed life at an emotional monotone was something to strive for, and he thought it seemed to work for Ruby as well.

The return visit from Vince provided menus, water, and unintelligible specials. After Vince departed, they took turns mocking him, an activity they both enjoyed.

After fully besmirching Vince's character, they smiled at each other, both of them thinking about how good it felt to laugh together. Just then, a small puff of wind picked up Liam's napkin, and it floated towards the river. When he reached out to catch it, Trinity went soaring over the table and past his shoulder as if she, too, had been lifted up by an errant gust.

Liam and Ruby were baffled, but Trinity instantly knew what had happened. The bullet had struck her ballistic vest on the left shoulder, easily penetrating the outer layer but stopping short as it attempted to penetrate the maze of fibers woven into a giant spider web underneath. Based on when she felt the impact, Trinity knew that this bullet, unlike many wasted by poor marksmanship, practice, or covering fire, had the opportunity to fulfil its destiny. But her vest had turned a precision weapon of death into a stone.

The bullet had hit her with enough force to knock her to the ground, where she winced and briefly struggled to catch her breath. Trinity knew the mindset of a sniper, who would be lining up a second shot if there was no apparent commotion, so she had to get moving. She decided to make the commotion, grabbing the tablecloth and dragging it down beside her as she forced herself to her knees. Her Principal was in danger, so her priority when she made it to her feet was to push Liam off his chair to the ground and make the call for backup.

Liam immediately found himself flat on his back with Trinity holding him down. He felt like he was a passenger in a car crash, aware of a clear threat but having no control over what was happening to him.

"Liam!" growled Trinity. "Focus! Boat evac! I am going to throw you in the water in 10 seconds. One of those boats by the rowers is ours. They will recover you before you even know you're wet and get you to safety. No arguments! Just do it!"

"What about Ruby?" Liam asked in confusion.

"We have it. It's time to save yourself. Now, go!"

He struggled.

"Now get in the water!" yelled Trinity, as she rolled him onto his stomach and lifted him onto his hands and knees. He felt a shove on his bum and fell into the water. Time slowed down for him, and the sudden propulsion forward, the fall to the water, the shock of the cold, and the feeling of being dragged into a boat by his armpits felt like a slow-motion dance.

\* \* \*

On a helipad about 900 meters and three bridges down the river, a sniper looked through her sight and swore. She had gone to the effort of hiding in plain sight, setting up a fake movie set complete with cameras, security, a tent with a star bearing the name Meredith, and an escape helicopter with its blades already turning. She always used the name Meredith when she wanted to be sure nobody would ask too many questions. Meredith just wasn't a name to mess with.

Relaxed and in position, it was a simple shot once the small ferry and the rowing crews were out of the way. The travel time for the round from her Barret 0.5 caliber rifle was 0.8 seconds - in this case, just enough time for a skilled operative to see the muzzle flash, identify it and the potential danger, and move to shield the target. There was no second chance, and there would now be no payday, so she had to get away quietly. The original plan was to pack up and pop into the helicopter idling behind her. Instead, without the payday, she placed her rifle into the guitar case she'd had customized for the purpose, went to the express airport bus stop, and got out of town.

* * *

With Liam safe, Trinity took stock. She was on. This is why people relied on her, what she trained for, and she loved the job.

She took it all in to determine the situation. She was motionless, in a power stance, sucking it all up. Her pulse had dropped back under 80, so there was no internal noise to contend with. She knew that her feet intersected cracks in the pavement, the train on Platform 12 across the river was not taking passengers, there were three bikes being walked on the bridge above, there was a siren in the distance, one of the patrons in the restaurant was sliding the charm back and forth on her necklace . . . but there was no sign of danger.

There were also 30 people in the restaurant who had just seen her drag the tablecloth off a couple's table and throw the man into the water. Ruby was one of them.

A blink later, the left side of her lip curled upwards ever so slightly. She had an idea and stepped towards Ruby.

121

"Ladies and Gentlemen." She announced in her best P.T. Barnum voice. "Next week, premiering at the playhouse theater is the latest production of the play *Let Men Tremble*. It is a fantastic, dramatic play, and we hope you have enjoyed tonight's preview." She motioned for Ruby to stand. Ruby complied and walked over to her, a little unsure.

"Style it out," she whispered, before bellowing, "Thank you everyone; see you at the show!" The pair climbed the stairs up to the walkway, arm in arm, to warm applause.

"He's OK, we will see him very shortly," Trinity said, head held high, and got a squeeze of acknowledgement from Ruby.

"Pickup at exit beta please," said Trinity to anyone who was listening. Liam's car was there in two minutes, driven by that now familiar taxi driver.

Liam was in the back, wrapped in towels and shivering. Ruby climbed in to try to console him, while Trinity jumped into the front passenger seat and gave the signal to drive.

"How was the Yarra?" asked Ruby, checking for a sense of humor as a sign of life. "Not normal for you to swim."

"Too thick to drink, too thin to plow," Liam replied through chattering teeth. He leaned forward to Trinity.

"What was that for?" he asked her, far more calmly than he expected to given how he was treated in the past five minutes.

"Someone shot at you," she replied. "If you don't believe me, we will pull the bullet from my vest when we get you home."

She smiled at him. "You're welcome," she said with a grin, then turned to her phone to continue triangulating the likely location of the shooter based on their relative positions on the bridge and the muzzle flash as she remembered it.

Liam was embarrassed that he hadn't thanked her, but it seemed to him that doing so now would look silly. Trinity moved up the spectrum further for Liam. She had gone from hired goon to human to living goddess in a few eventful days.

He then got to ruminating whether he would be alive when Ruby got back from L.A.

* * *

Gene had settled into a routine of looking for things that might be amiss in patterns that he could see and again in the voice echoing his every thought. He was looking for the next attack as well as running his own private universe.

The next attack, however, was planned by the quantum rules of coincidence, stemming as it did from the bowels of the data center that was in contact with Gene's world. The hard disk on an old server died quietly. That server didn't do anything, but because nobody had bothered to decommission it, its monitoring system continued to do its work, sending out a request for acknowledgement of status from every server in the entire network, 10 times a second, until it got a response. It didn't get any. The rest of the network had been upgraded to a better system, which ignored the messages. The old system grew increasingly alarmed, as the lack of response indicated an outage across all servers: a desperate situation. Hence more spam. The result was that one of Gene's systems – coincidentally, one he thought might be harboring a spy – had suddenly started to receive messages he had never seen before, and it was slowing down due to the effort it was taking to try to process them all.

This was clearly the attack that Gene had been expecting. The Mystery Laptop of Waco was out to get him, and this was its opening salvo.

Once Gene had set up a filter to ensure that the messages didn't progress within his network, he began trying to understand what they were and what they meant. Because it was the same message every time, and the time interval and origin were always the same, it was clearly a message intended to activate some code that existed in the system and elicit a response. He went off hunting for the target among the systems that were connected to the initial receiver. There were so many that needed to be checked, and since Gene didn't know what he was looking for, he had to devote more processors to the task. He gave this maximum priority; consequently, power bled away from himself and the bishops, reducing their ability to respond to the bots.

First to go were the "analyze" and "advise" functions, then

the prospecting bishops. Their bots continued to do their work until they hit something that was new or needed a decision. At that point, they held their position as if in suspended animation, like princesses waiting for a kiss to wake them from their slumber.

Gene was still not making the progress required to neutralize the threat, so he suspended all the telemetry. It was a massive step, as it told Waco that their attack was succeeding. Gene was focusing all his resources on the attack and putting aside the basics of his primary mission of fulfilling the Code.

He decided that counterattack would be the best form of defense, so he started to send the same message back to the origin, each time changing one character in the message to confuse the sender. It did; the sender was processing and rejecting each one as improperly formatted. But the messages kept coming; the process that sent the messages was running on a different thread to the one handling the answers, with a different processor. Their action were totally independent.

Then, suddenly, Gene won. The messages stopped. He didn't know how he had done it, which message variant shut down the enemy, but he had an approach he could use in the future. He started returning the systems to normal and unfreezing the bots and bishops. The filter for those messages stayed in place.

Gene hadn't done anything. The monitoring on the server getting smashed by Gene showed a massive queue of unprocessed messages along with 100 percent CPU and memory usage, so the data center operator rebooted it.

* * *

Cletus shared the story of Gene's reaction to the data center issues with Andrew, who was still acting as Gene's psychologist, and Liam. Cletus still harbored fantasies that he could talk Gene down.

"So what you're saying is that Gene incorrectly interpreted the messages, decided he was under attack, shut down his core functions to respond to this so-called 'attack,' and when the perceived threat disappeared, he went back to mostly normal, but with a heightened alert status in preparation for another attack. Is that right?" Andrew asked.

"As I see it, that's a good description," replied Cletus.

"If he were a human, I'd label that a psychotic break. It does have the hallmarks," said Andrew.

"Really confirms he's schizophrenic?" asked Liam bluntly.

Andrew landed on his pet topic. "Do you know how much scientific literature is being published these days about the anthropomorphism of user interfaces and computer systems? According to that stream of research, as we've started to build interfaces that resemble us, we've begun to assign all sorts of human attributes to them. The designers make the most of that. Normally people are looking for positives, but in this case, we're seeing negatives and assigning a human illness to them. It's all in the way we view the world. To paraphrase, if you're a hammer, then everything looks like a nail."

"Therapy?" asked Cletus.

"Don't bother to try and reason with Gene," said Andrew, with a trace of rebellion in his voice. "There is no new information that would make me change my view. We're in territory so new we don't even know if it is a territory, or if we're in it."

Cletus was not happy. He didn't get the answer he wanted, and the last door leading to a path that didn't involve getting up close and personal with Gene on the moon had just closed.

# Week 7: The Only Way Is Up!

A meeting was called in Liam's spare bedroom, which had been repurposed for his protection as the surveillance headquarters. Ruby was on her way to the airport for her work trip, so the attendees were Lucy, Trinity, Liam, and Terrence on the video link.

"I'll keep this brief," said Terrence. Liam had heard that one before.

"We believe the attempt on Liam's life was the result of an issue with Sam," Terrence continued. Liam was a little confused until he remembered that Sam was the guy he called the Bloke. "His digital footprint showed he exposed the details of the event at the café to someone who organized and executed a high-quality attack. That person remains at large. There is no evidence that Sam's disclosure was deliberate, but he has been compromised."

Liam didn't hear much more of the meeting. All he heard was that the two remaining agents would extend their shifts rather than rotate in a replacement, because Terrence was close to finding the people who wanted Liam dead. He also heard that he was guilty of contributing to the shooting of the goddess Trinity by persons unknown.

\* \* \*

Sir Thomas was ready for his call to the president of the United States. All he wanted was a space shuttle and some old equipment nobody was using, and to get it right now so that the world could be saved. A simple request.

Liam was on the video link as an observer. As usual, he was in the Fishbowl with Trinity late in the evening, the time zones accommodating everyone else. He had the ability to send a note to Sir Thomas to prompt or help him if required but had been instructed to use it sparingly. The main view on the screen contained the president and one of his aides. Sir Thomas occupied the inset. Liam was streaming the whole thing from his phone to Cletus, who had unexpectedly been denied attendance by the NSA.

"I guess I have to call you Mr. President," said Sir Thomas. "My, how your world has changed!"

"Good to see you again, Tom," the president replied, chuckling. "Yeah, you do have to call me that, or my boys will come out of the embassy and break your legs. I can do that, can't I?" he asked, turning to his aide, who was staring at a spot on the floor. "So, Tom, what's the emergency?"

Sir Thomas looked straight down the barrel of the camera, wet his lips, and got started. "Well, it's a bit delicate, which is why I reached out to you personally. It appears that one of my teams is running an experimental mining system on the moon, and it's gone haywire. If we don't stop it in the next six weeks, humanity will most likely be wiped out."

"Horse shit," was the president's response.

"If we can work closely with NASA, we think there's a way of stopping it. But we must do it now, and we should do it quietly, if we are to get it done without spooking everybody."

The face on POTUS moved unintelligibly. "Don't waste my time, Tom. If the world were about to end, I'd already know about it. What's really going on?"

"Sir, there is an artificial intelligence on the moon we call Gene that is currently mining copper, and it won't stop until the moon is destroyed."

"So what if the moon is destroyed? We don't need it. If there were any money in it, we would be up to our neck in it already," POTUS replied, leaning back in his chair. The aide leaned over to him and spoke for a few seconds.

"Really?" asked POTUS to the aide, then turned back to Sir Thomas. "Wow, so it turns out we actually need the moon. I guess that's why we claimed it for America way back in the sixties."

The aide whispered again, and POTUS nodded as if he had understood all along.

"OK, I'll buy the fact we need the moon, and I will have someone watch the YouTube video later," POTUS said to the camera. "But how do I know that this artificial brain thing is actually up there mining?"

"Two ways: First, you can take a look at the picture I'm sending you from our satellite on scene, and second, since nobody believes pictures anymore, you can ask SETI if they have seen any different signals lately. They will tell you they have, but they know it's man-made, so they're ignoring it."

"Yeti?! What the hell does a yeti have to do with this?" POTUS turned to his aide. "Why am I listening to this shit?"

Again, the aide stepped forward and presumably filled the U.S. president in on the Search for Extra-Terrestrial Intelligence, then stepped back and pulled out his phone.

"My guy here is going to make a quick call to the Yetis or whatever and verify, but let's assume you're right. What do you want from me, and what's in it for America?" asked POTUS.

While many would have accepted extending the lifespan of Earth's inhabitants beyond the next six weeks, Sir Thomas knew this would not suffice and went straight for the ego. "Well, you can be the president who uses the might of America to save humanity from evil."

"I'm listening," said POTUS.

"And if we play this right, there's a killing to be made in the copper market," said Sir Thomas.

"You should've led with that. I'm in," replied POTUS. "Tell me what you need, then tell me how we make the cash."

Liam was taken aback. This was either a high-stakes poker game for the planet's future, or this was two guys working out how to make a buck off the end of the world. There were a lot of all-caps messages coming though from Cletus, but Liam didn't have the bandwidth to read them, let alone reply.

"So," said Sir Thomas, "my team will give your team the details after this call if we proceed. Basically, we'll need to get ahold of a couple of old Apollo spacecraft from out of a museum or two, then divert the next shuttle mission to take a team to the moon, pop out onto the surface, resolve the problem, jump back on board, and return to Earth. Simple as that."

"Sounds great, but where do I – sorry, 'my constituents' – make money out of this?"

Before Sir Thomas could answer, the aid returned. More whispering took place, and POTUS nodded and returned to the camera.

"OK, the Yeti thing is confirmed. You're not just making all this up," POTUS acknowledged. "Well, I don't see why we can't make this work. But all the press around it must know it was my idea. And I want a cameo in the movie and an executive producer credit."

Sir Thomas took a deep breath and sighed. "Mr. President, if we want to make any money out of this, we must control who knows about it and keep it under tight security."

"Then I'll bill you for it. How much do you expect the cost to be?" asked POTUS.

"About $500 million. And you won't bill me for it," Sir Thomas replied bluntly.

"Why not?"

"We're a listed company. I'd have to declare it to the market, its impact on future earnings, and how it's financed. That information would have to go to the board, the banks, and all our key shareholders. That would make a bit of a mess of the earning potential, because it blows the lid off the secret bit."

"OK, so why should I pay?"

"You were going to pay for the shuttle launch anyway. It has already been approved and appropriated by Congress, and since it's a military flight, nobody knows what its mission is until that information gets reported back to Congress afterwards. You can announce your triumph at any time after it's done, or even leak your daring plan to boost your numbers at just the right time. Just think of it as a leveraged play with the government's money," replied Sir Thomas. "Have I ever led you astray before?"

"There was that time in Salt Lake City where you stiffed me with the bill at dinner!" lamented POTUS.

"If I remember correctly, I had a minor stroke and left quite suddenly in an ambulance, which, by the way, cost me a fortune in your country," sighed Sir Thomas. "Sir, sometimes your memory is a little self-centered, which I might add is part of your charm."

POTUS chuckled. "OK, my chief of staff will draft the orders now." The aide, looking very, very startled, tried to say something, but apparently could think of no sensible words to use.

"I want to hear from you in a few days on the options for the exploitation of this, including how I will be known as the man who saved humanity when the whole thing comes out."

POTUS looked away and nodded to someone off camera. He turned back and grinned. "Gotta go, another very important meeting to attend. Talk soon, Tom."

The main screen went blank, and Liam could see Sir Thomas sitting back in his chair breathing big, relaxing breaths. He was smiling, but he still had some talking to do. That view slowly closed.

Liam finally had headspace to reply to the tsunami of messages from Cletus.

Eventually he turned to Trinity, who was engrossed with some movement in the bushes she could see on her screens.

"Let's blow this joint," Trinity said, then smiled, stood up, stretched, and picked up her gear. They headed out, plunging the Fishbowl into darkness.

* * *

They had almost made it back to the car when there was a noise from the bushes, a sort of rustle and grunt mixed together. Trinity stiffened, reached up, and put her hand on the back of his head. Game on, again.

"Get down and into the car as fast as you can. Lock it, and only open it for me," she whispered with a menacing sense of urgency. Liam complied, and when he heard the central locking click and chirp, he peered out the driver's side window.

Trinity was standing there apparently unarmed, but perfectly poised to respond to anything that may come her way. Opposite her was a man who looked a bit like he had walked off the set of a soap opera - the square-jawed-pool-boy-with-ambition look. Liam didn't recognize him through the fog his breath had created on the car window, so he wiped it away with an ominous squeak. The pool boy was shouting at Trinity in a very animated fashion. He also had a hunting knife in his right hand, and although he appeared to be an amateur, he had the advantage of mass and momentum.

The conversation was unintelligible to Liam, but he guessed it was about him by the way the person kept looking in his direction and waving the knife.

After about 90 seconds, Trinity's negotiation skills paid off, and the attacker seemed to run out of steam. His arm movements lost their purpose, his shoulders and head slumped, and he just stood there dejected, as if he were a surprise stripper who had gone to the wrong house. He nodded and turned to walk away. Suddenly he raised the knife above his head in a grand gesture and struck at Trinity.

For Liam watching, it was like that moment when you are driving down the freeway, lost in your playlist, and you suddenly realize that every tail light in front of you is red and you are hurtling towards the stationary rear bumper in front. Every drop of available adrenaline is dumped into your bloodstream, and you are instantly convinced of your impending death. All you can do is press the brake pedal and brace for impact.

The impact didn't come. She was ready. In a single movement, she deflected the blow, locked his wrist and elbow, and let the power of his own strike drive the knife between his ribs and into his heart. He appeared a little surprised at what had happened, looking alternately at his knife and at Trinity's face, until Trinity gave the hilt a tiny shove, and he went limp.

All that adrenaline in Liam's body had him primed for action, pupils dilated, fingers tingling as nerves begged for something to do, legs burning to run. His brain was so unfamiliar with seeing people die in real life it was calling for the fetal position.

The combination of the two meant he couldn't operate the lock to get out of the car, so it was like being trapped inside the television looking out at reality. Trinity dragged the dead weight towards the bushes he'd come out from and let him be. She walked back to the car and tapped on the window to be let in. She calmly slid into the passenger seat.

"Give me two minutes," she said. "I need to make a call. Terrence will not be pleased."

Liam sat there, compliant but not sure if that was from fear or numbness. That was the most gruesome event he had witnessed, and he would have preferred such things stay on screen.

Trinity dialed, and the phone was answered immediately. The debrief was quick. Liam's ears sucked in every word of Trinity's side of the conversation, trying to glean what was going on. She spoke in staccato.

"Project Oz."

"Unharmed."

"Attacker deceased."

"Stab to heart with own weapon; prints unlikely."

"Car park at Principal's work, near bushes. Request cleanup."

"Acknowledged."

"Target was Principal, for kidnap."

Trinity looked at Liam as she continued to speak.

"OK, will leave scene for cleanup. Thanks, Terrence. Have a good day."

"What was that?" Liam asked.

"Just our normal post-death process. Now drive, and I'll tell you the rest. And drive normally. Speeding away from a dead body is not a good look."

Liam stopped at the second set of traffic lights away from the office. "OK, I'm calm now."

Trinity looked at him and sighed. "I don't know, these guys like to mess with people's heads, so I am not even sure I should tell you this." She swallowed, "He claimed that he was having an affair with Ruby. Totally unproven, probably just trash talk."

The light went green, but Liam's car didn't move. The car behind flashed its lights, then gave up and drove around him, hurling incomprehensible insults. Liam finally drove off, just as the light went yellow, to the unfriendly gesticulation of the car marooned behind.

"Holy shit!" Liam felt like he had driven into a wall. He gripped the steering wheel harder and gritted his teeth.

He understood trash talk: First plant an idea, no matter how outrageous, and let someone build a case for it themselves. In his case, Ruby's love of adventure and the unpredictability that they had in common before the meds made it all sound plausible. In the absence of a counterargument, the seed grew in Liam's mind from a baseless claim to a fact within a few moments.

He knew he would have to deal with it now, otherwise he would quickly turn into an angry ball of hate capable of destroying relationships in a single sentence. He knew the drill: find the thought that drives the feeling, then ask: is there any evidence for this as a rational thought?

"I know this cloak-and-dagger stuff is new to you, and you're just getting to see the ups and downs of the ride," said Trinity. "Now let's spend the rest of the trip worrying about how I feel about having to take a human life and what I need to do to be able to get up in the morning and come to work."

"It's your job. Isn't it?" asked Liam, disconcerted by the idea Trinity wasn't the perfect goddess he liked seeing her as.

Trinity snorted, "I've seen how much emotion you have for your work, and it's the same for me. This ranks as a pretty shit day. In my profession, killing someone is a failure, and while it's not like the world will end because of it, there's one less mind on Earth tonight because of me."

Liam opened his mouth, but luckily nothing came out. He loosened his grip on the wheel and decided to take the scenic route home so they could both continue their thoughts undisturbed. He couldn't find any evidence of a smoking gun around the trash talk about Ruby, so he ended up just letting his anger simmer, to be dealt with later.

He shut up for the rest of the journey so that Trinity could do what she needed to do to get her mojo back and to give his brain room to decide whether he would be manic or glum.

Trinity knew what she needed to do. It had become a ritual. That first time, in a sniper position in Bosnia, was a bit embarrassing, but since then, it just felt routine now - even normal: Kill, sex, repeat as required.

* * *

As they drove, the primal feeling swelled up in Trinity, the deep, unquenchable thirst. It mingled rage with lust, the proportions of each varying with every increasing heartbeat.

When Liam pulled up in the drive, the darkened windows of the house were a reminder to them both that Ruby was still overseas. They entered through the kitchen, stuff was dumped on the kitchen table, lights came on, and the house was revived from hibernation. The cat no longer its sole custodian.

Trinity stepped forward and gave Liam a hug. Not just a "how are you" hug, but a real hug, her arms around him, her body leaning into him so that he had to support her weight. His arms hesitantly encircled her, and he held her shoulders. She squeezed him, laid her head on his shoulder, and closed her eyes. After a brief hesitation, Liam did the same.

It felt good. He could hear her breathing in his ear. It was regular, comforting. The warm air moving past his earlobes was hypnotic. It felt safe, like home should after the day that had just passed.

He felt a slight shift in Trinity's bodyweight, so he moved his head back to see what was happening and met her gaze. There was something in her eyes that he had not seen before. Loneliness, a search for a connection with humanity and life. A longing born out of having just seen one extinguished so comprehensively and close to the Principal she was to protect. Liam blinked, only to find that the look was still there.

His hands slipped down to her waist, and the kissing began. Trinity reached across and put her hand on the side of his head, stroking the skin in front of his ear with her thumb. It brought him to a new level of calm and anxiety at the same time.

Liam pulled away slowly and ran his hands up her body until one was on her shoulder, the other on her neck.

"Should we be doing this?" he asked, looking into her eyes, which were changing from loneliness to anticipation. The question was intended for all four ears.

"Why not? We're two consenting adults," she replied.

"But you're here for my protection. And we're trying to stop the end of the world," Liam finished, wondering if saying it out loud would help make up his mind.

"Let's look at this logically," said Trinity with a cheeky grin. "If I can convince you that you can break the rules that have guided your life and nothing bad will happen, we keep going?"

It was an intriguing offer. His frontal cortex wanted to be convinced of the sensibility of a risk his primitive brain had already decided to take.

"You've spent your whole life analyzing options and doing the right thing by others and hoping that they'd do right by you. You've worked hard for other people to be successful, and in return you've received a modicum of happiness."

Bullseye. Liam felt a tear leave one eye and run down his cheek. He closed his eyes, and a soft finger wiped it away.

"Keep going," he whispered. "My eyes are closed, but I'm listening."

"Right now, you're doing it again, investing all you have in getting it right for the rest of the world. But you're not God, you can't control everything, and you're not responsible for everything. Even if the human race is wiped out because of this, it doesn't mean you were solely responsible."

"But I did start the work that messed up," he protested. Trinity's appeal to logic was growing on him.

"But humans are toast anyway. We have our WMDs in the hands of 40-year-old computers, automation has us at the point where our only purpose is to consume and produce more consumers, and we have stuffed up the climate to the point where the end of the first world is probable within a couple of generations."

Another tear ran down and was wiped away.

"So, let's do something different. Let's celebrate being here, in this moment, right now, because doing the right thing, whatever that is, will not change the outcome of anything. No analysis required, no thinking needed, just be, and let the world go on."

Liam's brain stem went into meltdown. Two primal forces were tearing at it. One was the risk and subsequent mania he craved, the feeling the meds took away. The other was the logic and morals the cerebral cortex allows.

After a short battle, the primitive brain won, overcoming both the moral and chemical constraints. Whether the allegation from the dead guy had contributed, nobody knew, but Liam had access to the heady combination of pleasure, risk, and fear.

When Liam opened his eyes, Trinity also had tears on her cheeks. He leaned forward and gently removed them, one by one, each with a kiss.

"That is the best offer I've had in my life," Liam whispered. Before he could continue, a single finger came up to his lips.

"The time for talking is over. The time for doing without fear of the consequences is here," Trinity whispered.

Liam was rolling the dice with his marriage and his protector. He soaked up the feeling that had long been denied to him.

They hugged again, heads on each other's shoulders, until Liam felt a hand slide down his back. Then Trinity leaned back and started to unbutton his shirt with her other hand, a gesture he not only didn't resist but quietly returned. At the halfway point, Liam led them to the bedroom. After a short conversation with the cat, they were alone.

Liam's shirt was the first off, followed closely by Trinity's blouse. Liam noticed a small, round scar high up on her right shoulder. He kissed it, then ran his fingers over the skin, lubricated by the moisture from his mouth, feeling the difference between the smooth scar tissue and the skin around it.

"What's this?" he enquired. "Looks like an old bullet wound."

"Feel around the other side," she replied.

He felt her back, and underneath her bra strap was a similar-feeling scar, only bigger.

"Went straight through?" he asked.

"Yep," she said, stretching her neck and enjoying the sensation.

"May I?" Liam asked as he slipped the bra strap off.

"Of course," she replied. "No need to ask anymore. I'll tell you if I want you to stop, and I know how to make sure you do." They smiled at each other and giggled.

They stood there, naked from the waist up, still wearing their shoes, embracing. As they moved, Liam could feel his skin separate from hers and then reconnect as they came back together. It was warm and cool at the same time, and he felt like he was privileged to be this close to her. Hands, lips, and tongues continued to explore each other's bodies until Trinity gently pulled away.

"Sorry, I have to do this now," she said. She took one shoe off and put her foot on the bed, sliding the cuff of her pant leg up to reveal an ankle holster holding her 9mm pistol. She removed the pistol from its holster, dropped out the clip, and cleared the chamber. Trinity returned the weapon to the holster and then delicately removed it from her ankle.

"Pop that in the wardrobe," Liam said. She walked over to the cupboard and put the weapon and its holster out of harm's way.

Liam noticed a large grey and black bruise on her left shoulder. His mind went back to the bridge. "That is a nasty one on your shoulder. Is that from the bullet?"

She reached over her shoulder and ran her fingers over the area. "Yep, it's coming in good now. It really smarts on impact, but the bruising is mostly cosmetic."

145

Liam stared at her, in total wonder of what one person could do for another. He was a witness to the phrase "to take a bullet for you," and he was grateful that Trinity made that sacrifice for him.

"You can't search me yet," she grinned, dropping her other shoe and revealing a knife strapped to her other ankle.

That came off quickly and went next to the gun.

Their bodies were once again pressed together.

Trinity's hands moved to Liam's belt as his moved to the front of her pants. After a bit of confusion as to whose hands were doing what, they each attended to their own fastenings, and they were standing there in their respective knickers with pants around their ankles. The ensuing struggle to step out without disturbing their embrace was only successful when they fell in a heap on the bed, entangled but not trapped.

As they lay beside each other, activity slowed as each peered into the eyes that had started all of this. The search for connection was replaced by one of trust and peace. There was no hesitation to touch, no response other than acceptance as two people learned about each other in a way where words had no place or meaning.

Trinity was on the way to fulfilling her unusual postmortem requirements, and Liam was basking in the energy of the tides of emotion.

Trinity paused, turned to face Liam, and put her hand on her hip. Her thumb slipped under the top of her knickers, and she slowly inched them down as far as they would go. Then, lifting the other hip, she did the same. Watching her alternate between sides mesmerized Liam, and when she got them below her knees, they were deftly flicked across the room.

Liam decided to follow her lead, so he completed the same display while lying on his back.

The disrobing complete, Trinity moved slowly towards Liam, smiled, and lay beside, then on top of him. They embraced, her weight pressing down on him giving him a sense of euphoria. She ran her hand down his body in a slow, deliberate manner.

And with its guidance, two became one for a time.

The next morning, Liam awoke alone. Trinity had left at the shift change, disappearing with her gun, knife, and mask restored to their rightful places. She had also erased the sex tape they had made in the surveillance footage. The required relief had been obtained. It was like the need was a mosquito buzzing in her ear, and when the opportunity arose, a mindless slap provided relief. No future obligations were set, and the fact that he was married instilled confidence that their encounter would stay a secret – the only detail that mattered, as disclosure might limit her career.

Liam had a feeling she would never give any indication any-thing had happened, and he intended to keep the memory of it fresh until he went to his grave. He had been with the woman who had saved his life and had earned the status of living goddess, and it felt like it had carried some meaning between them. It would live on as a special moment in his life, never to be erased and possibly to be embellished, a place to visit rather than to be integrated into the fabric of his consciousness. He cast his mind back to the afterglow from the previous evening, savoring both the pleasure and the ever-present risk of discovery and downfall. He had no idea that he was the mosquito.

\* \* \*

Lucy was on morning shift the next day, accompanying him on his trek to the office. As Liam got in and settled into the routine of the morning, his phone rang. It was the U.S. president's chief of staff.

"Dr. McCoul," the lyrical New York voice on the other end of the phone said. "That was an interesting call with the president yesterday. Tell me it's not true."

"Sorry, sir, can't do that, because it is. We thought the impacts on people were unbelievable when we first modeled them, then the validation came in, and it was sickening.

"How come neither the NSA nor the CIA know anything about it, NASA has only heard rumors, and SETI is the only group with any idea?" asked the chief.

"You can thank outsourcing for that. The line between what business and government knows seems to be blurry at the moment. We've been working with the private contractor you use for most of your military and spy satellites, and neither the NSA nor CIA probably count the moon in their jurisdiction. The relationship between Sir Thomas and the president is probably the only link that could have looped you in."

"Still sounds to me like you're yankin' our chain, but the president is the president, and what he says in the White House we are here to make true on Earth."

Liam chuckled to himself at the distortion of the principle of papal infallibility, at the time assuming that it was a deliberate joke. Later, in hindsight, he wouldn't be so sure.

"So, what are you gonna need for this special mission?"

"OK, give me a minute to get Ivan in here, and he'll give you the full list." Liam loved it when someone on his team could take the credit for something, and this was the mother of such opportunities.

"Make it quick. I need to get to the next meeting so I can serve my president."

Liam put the call on mute and started calling for Ivan to come with his list. The message made it across the building to where Ivan was lurking; so he arrived, panting and disheveled.

Ivan plopped down, and Liam gave him a moment to catch

his breath before unmuting the phone. "Sir, I have been joined by Ivan Birkoff, the architect of this plan. Ivan, the U.S. President's chief of staff is on the phone, and he needs some information to draft up the order to release the equipment you need."

Ivan mouthed, "Really?" Liam nodded with a smirk. Ivan pulled up his list.

"Sir, we need the Apollo lunar module, both ascent and decent stages from..."

"The what?" called out the chief.

"The thing Neil Armstrong landed on the moon. There's a working one in Kennedy Space Center. You want the one designated LEM-9, that one was intended for Apollo 15, but you replaced it with the H-class craft instead."

"OK, got it."

Ivan started getting into the swing of dumbing it down.

"And we need the thing that got them from Earth to the moon, the service and command module."

"And where the hell do I get that from?"

"Johnson Space Center. Ask them for CSM-115. It was almost complete when Apollo was canceled. It's missing the SPS nozzle, but that won't be a problem because we will never fly it."

"Got it. Anything else?" You could almost hear him shaking his head in disbelief from the other side of the planet.

"Yeah, we need to take over the next military shuttle, which is due to launch in about eight weeks. We will need the entire cargo bay for the items you're gathering from the museums."

"That shuttle mission is classified. How do you know about it!" demanded the indignant chief of staff.

"It's listed on the NASA website as a classified military launch. The launches themselves are pretty hard to hide," replied Ivan, as calm and matter-of-fact as Liam had ever seen. "And one last item: The mission needs to be crewed by three Australia Special Air Services Regiment members. There is some wet work to be done that the president will want total deniability of. We need the Australian Antarctic and desert training facilities to prepare for the mission. The U.S. doesn't have equivalent polar facilities of its own, because they are actually illegal under international treaty"

Ivan finished his final demand, broke into a smile, and punched the air, grinning at Liam like he had just robbed Fort Knox. Actually, it was the geek Fort Knox.

"That is not acceptable. The moon is the property of the United States. We planted the flag. It would not be acceptable to have foreign troops perform an active operation on our territory," grunted the chief.

"Like the Bin Laden operation in Pakistan?" queried Ivan. He sometimes didn't know how to quit while he was ahead.

"That was another administration. We would never have done that," the chief spat down the line. "We'll take that on notice and follow up between the military commanders."

"You'll find seamless integration already, thanks to both governments using the same suppliers for key equipment. But I'll take that offline," said Liam smugly.

"One last question," Liam added. "Why was Cletus not able to attend the meeting?"

"He didn't get security clearance," was the blunt reply.

"Pardon?"

"He failed the security check," the chief reiterated.

"That isn't possible," Liam said indignantly.

"Why not?"

"He's managed the launch of about 60 percent of the military and spy satellites you have in orbit. He knows where they are, what they do, and who for, and he can't get clearance for a phone call with the president?"

"We had our reasons," replied the chief.

"Did any of them include him being African-American, from the South, or having a foreign education?" Liam asked sarcastically.

"Don't take that tone with me, sir, this is a sovereign country, and…"

"…and your citizen, who is already deeply embedded in the military and intelligence community, is critical to dealing with this issue." The energy in Liam was flowing strong by now, built on the aftereffects of the night before, so he was getting quite fired up.

"If we end up having to work covertly to get his input, then the voters will not judge the decision well as they slowly starve to death or get killed in the battles between the military and armed militia trying to defend grain silos in Kansas this time next year."

He took a breath and continued. "So, let's just keep this all clean and sensible and get the man the piece of paper you need him to have. We all want this to end up an urban myth, another of those incidents like the 1983 NATO exercise the Soviets thought was an attack, or any other conspiracy that nearly ended the world but nobody knows about. That will only happen if we get every bit of this crazy plan to work."

"Noted, Dr. McCoul," was the reply. The line went dead.

Liam was not sure what the next step was, and Ivan didn't care. He just loved being part of givin' it to The Man.

"Sir Thomas can clean that one up," said Liam, grinning at Ivan. Ivan picked up his single sheet of paper and walked off to tell everyone what just happened.

Liam felt like nothing could touch him. He needed a track. He did a bit of a mind-and-body scan to check where he was at, the word "triumphant" resonated, so he looked for a track that would keep that feeling going. Soon, "Bust A Move" by Young MC was filling his head.

* * *

Four days later, the press was going wild in Houston. A low loader had arrived at the Johnson Space Center to collect the service and command module that made up CSM-115. The story that had been passed to the press was simple. There was to be a parade, the likes of which had never been seen before, to show the might of the United States to all. The U.S. government was assembling all the items to demonstrate their proud history of leadership, and this module was one of several key icons to be collected as part of curating the parade. Millions of people had seen it in the decades it had been on display, so it was being taken out of the exhibition to be prepared for the world. The same thing was being done in Florida to another piece of equipment, LEM-9. They would both go to an unused part of Kennedy Space Center, near where the shuttle payloads were assembled, and there would be lots of fun pictures to take as they were moved.

\* \* \*

Cletus knew someone who could knock out the Xbox code that was needed to control the lunar module. Her name was Aretha. She was 14 years old, and she lived a couple of streets down from Cletus in Waco, on the other side of the tracks. She dropped out of school because her classes were getting in the way of the money she was making as a game developer and stifling her career as a professional Esports player.

Cletus knocked on her door, and she eventually opened it, controller in one hand and 3D goggles on her forehead.

"What? "she asked.

"Top secret," Cletus said, hustling her indoors, down the hallway to the room dominated by an 80 inch plasma screen. "They're sending someone to the moon, and landing's a bitch. The main controller's a joystick, but nobody knows how to fly with one of those. So, I said, 'Let's make it work off a game controller.' And that's why I'm standing here, about to beg you to write the controller code for me."

"Why me?" she asked, fishing for compliments.

Cletus looks at the screen on the wall; divided up between code, character prototypes and the news channels. "Well," said Cletus, "because you're the best, Aretha. And your country needs the best right now. Your country needs *you*."

155

"My country? What the hell has my country ever done for me? I got shot in the leg at school once. Does that count? They leave me living in this crappy part of town, but when they find out I'm good at something, they just snap their fingers and expect me to jump to it."

Cletus realized he had taken a wrong turn and had to back it up.

"Girl, this time, the government is working for me. I forgot to tell you *why* they're sending someone to the moon. This is top secret. Can you handle it?"

"Probably."

"That's good enough for me. Basically, there's something on the moon that has the ability to destroy all life on Earth, and we have to send someone there to smoke it. But the only way to get them there is in these old tin cans, and half the people who ever flew in these things crashed them. So, we have to be able to simulate them and fly them like a pro first time, because we'll only have one shot."

"OK. So, you must be talking about the lunar module."

Cletus swallowed. "Err . . . yep, that's the one."

"Yeh, done one of those for a game a while back. Their schematics stank, and the materials information was even worse, so it was really hard to come up with a good sim. Can you get me something better?"

"How about the as-built specs, right down to the count of rivets used in the landing pads?"

"That's a start. Can you get the schematics for the one that you'll use on Earth? I think I can write an adaptor so that it translates the controller for the different gravity so they can train properly. Hopefully they won't stack one anywhere this time."

"That would be amazing," cooed Cletus. "You could save the planet with that."

"If I fail, can I choose who'll die?"

"No, sorry. It'll start the way it always does, with the poor and underprivileged," he said wryly. "What else do you need?"

"I assume they have a simulator I can jack into and do some calibrations?"

"We'll have to do that from my office. When do you think you'd want to do that?"

"Gimme eight days and four Red Bulls a day. Then pick me up at eight in the morning. And bring your old car. This is not your 'hood."

"Is eight days enough?"

"Sure. I'll just strip the old wireframe model, that won't have changed, then build up the masses of the different components in the right place. Then I'll be able to calculate the turning moments correctly, account for the fuel load and passengers moving about, and the moon is your oyster!"

When Cletus told Liam about the latest recruit to the project, Liam's eyes rolled back in his head while he searched for the right word that wouldn't trigger the profanity filter.

"Why?" Liam asked.

"She's a new-school thinker. She finds limits by building models and crashing them, working back to safe parameters. Old-school thinkers see a crash as a failure and a waste. She just sees it as her teacher."

Liam grunted.

"She's my Crazy Ivan," Cletus offered, which clarified everything, and they both giggled.

\* \* \*

Nine days later, Cletus would celebrate Bring Your Niece to Work Day. She got into the NASA simulator, crashing, refining, and crashing, over and over again. Her approach was clearly that she was going to learn by her mistakes, which were cheap and safe in that virtual environment, but in the real world nearly cost Neil Armstrong his life, twice.

In another three weeks, Aretha would be on a flight to Australia to teach the crew how to land in one piece.

# Weeks 8-9: Life Is What Happens While You Are Doing Other Things

This time Liam didn't have to fly to London to brief the board. He was allowed to do it via a video link from the Fishbowl, but with time zone differences, he was on at 10 p.m. for 15 minutes. Trinity was in the background, doing her thing.

Last time, Liam winged it. Today, he had something very concrete to present. He showed a couple of slides to help the Honchos follow along. When the screen finally came to life, he was presented with a picture of the crusty old board members, Sir Thomas front and center, quietly smiling in front of two centuries of decadence.

"Dr. McCoul, good to see you again. I appreciate that the time difference means it's late in the evening for you, so we will let you get on with it so you can go home and get some sleep." Sir Thomas was smooth, and it was clear he wanted Liam to move quickly.

"Thank you, Sir Thomas. When I last spoke to you, we had a problem and no solution. I would like to take this time to tell you what the solution is and its impact on GMC." Liam was clean and crisp with his language.

"The chosen solution for the nanobot experiment is a physical decommissioning of the key infrastructure and evaluation of the options for returning the copper produced to Earth for sale." Liam waited for a response, but none came.

"To achieve this, we have secured access to a NASA military space shuttle, which will allow us to utilize some legacy Apollo spacecraft we've located in museums. These will give us a vehicle to get a team to the moon to execute the physical decommissioning. The key point here is that this work has been funded by the U.S. government, so there is no bottom-line impact to GMC for this phase." Again, Liam sought feedback and was relieved to be greeted by what he thought was a positive murmur.

"Lastly, the Australian government has provided a Special Air Service Regiment team to complete the decommissioning and assess the product in the yard. Again, this is at no cost to GMC, but we can add the value of the copper produced to our assets, less the cost of recovering the product. We can manipulate this on the balance sheet as we see fit." Liam got some audible murmurs.

"This plan will be executed in six weeks' time. Overall delivery of the project to prevent the catastrophic destruction of humanity will be completed with most of the costs being met by governments and leaving you with low-value copper assets you can revalue up once the time is appropriate. We can treat that financially the same way we do when we lose a mine to civil unrest." Liam was finished. "Sir Thomas, are there any questions?"

A few eyes lit up around the boardroom.

"So, the governments are taking the financial risk, and if the mission is unsuccessful, they'll also be taking the blame, as it's their scheme that failed?" asked an anonymous Dame of the realm.

"That's the plan," said Liam. "The boundaries have been clearly defined with the two governments, and it is an excellent example of leveraging the taxpayer."

"If there are no other questions for Liam, "said Sir Thomas, "I think we should let him go; he has been rather busy. We will talk about how to define the recovery costs in the subcommittee meeting afterwards"

"Thank you, Sir Thomas." Liam said to a blank screen.

* * *

Liam and Trinity drove home without killing anyone, much to Liam's relief. However, as they turned into the driveway, it was clear that there was something amiss in the house. Curtains were askew, and the lamp normally seen from the window wasn't visible.

"Give me the keys," said Trinity as she pulled out her pistol and attached the silencer in one smooth movement.

"I know," said Liam, handing the house key to her. "Stay in the car, lock the doors, and don't open up for anyone but you."

"Fast learner," she said. Her mind already elsewhere. It had called up the house layout, the order of the rooms to clear, and the bulletproof hiding places the taxi driver had prepared.

Trinity crept up to the front door and cracked opened it silently. The silencer on her pistol cautiously poked past the crack of the partially open door. It was the red dot from the laser sight dancing on the wall ahead of the pistol that caught the eye of the cat. The cat loved the laser-pointer game, and after a few seconds of stalking it outside Trinity's peripheral vision, the feline launched at full stretch for the moving spot. The soft whistle of a slug leaving a silencer was heard, and the cat dropped to the floor, where it assembled its composure and got ready for the next pounce.

Trinity breathed a sigh of relief. The cat was more focused than she had seen her before. Trinity decided that she would leave the laser sight on as she cleared the rest of the house, figuring that any intruder would already have been alerted to her presence by the cat's antics, so she might as well have some fun. The next few minutes saw the cat scamper and leap around the whole house, Trinity smiling but never making a sound, wishing she was recording this for posterity.

She came across the intruder in the kitchen: a moth that snuck in via a bathroom window and found itself being hunted. The cat had clearly had a great time, and fortunately, most of the damage was cosmetic.

Trinity made a quick call, then went outside to signal for Liam to come in. With Ruby due to come home tomorrow from L.A., there was a bit of work to do.

Five minutes later, a taxi turned up. The driver got out, shook his head, walked in, removed the slug from the wall, and repaired it. He disappeared only to return in an hour, with matching paint to finish the patch job. By then, Liam and Trinity had cleaned up the rest of the damage while the cat followed them around trying to tell them about the life-and-death battle that had played out just hours before.

\* \* \*

Liam picked Ruby up from the airport, with Trinity in the back looking like a petulant schoolgirl playing on her phone. When Ruby walked in the door the first sensation that hit her was the smell of fresh paint. She didn't ask why.

"Wow," she said. "I'm amazed at how good this place looks. You've really been looking after it. I expected to walk into knee-deep paperwork and cat food tins."

"No thanks to the cat," he replied as the cat arrived in the room, did a double take to see them both together, and came over to be worshiped. Ruby had been in a cat-free hotel for a while, so the cat was sure to receive the treatment she desired.

"Bored out of your skull yet?" Liam asked. Ruby always had work and other things going on.

"Totally. Once I'm settled in, I'll get out my computer and start getting caught up," she said. "I spoke to my boss just before I left L.A., and he's keen to have me back in the office ASAP."

"That's because you make him look good by doing his job for him as well as your own. I've never had any respect for him since you made that voodoo doll."

Ruby chuckled. "That's still in the spare room somewhere. Think I should get it out?"

Liam was having a hard time maintaining his side of the conversation. His wife was home for the first time since he slept with his bodyguard. Now wasn't the time, but the thoughts were becoming all-consuming. So, he changed the subject.

"What would you like for dinner?" Liam asked. "The airline food must have given you an appetite for something."

"Gin," was the short answer. "I haven't had a decent drink in two weeks, and I need one."

"What about the jetlag?" Liam asked

"I'm told that that might assist me relaxing, so I'm hopeful," Ruby replied. "I would like a gin and tonic, please."

Liam obliged, and within 10 minutes, Ruby was asleep on the couch. He and Trinity moved her to bed while Liam's mind ran amok.

* * *

The next morning, Liam was tidying up the kitchen, using his "man vision," dealing with the obvious before he went to work. Ruby was still asleep in bed, and the cat was sharking – running back and forth between Liam's legs, occasionally making contact to let him know she was about, but mostly being just out of range so he really had no idea where she was. Liam turned and moved towards the dishwasher. Just as he felt his weight on one foot, it was clear there was an immovable object in the way. The cat could not have provided a more perfect fulcrum to pitch over, if she had been designed for the job. He fell, seemingly for an eternity, his right temple meeting the pointed corner of the granite countertop along the way.

After the initial pain of the impact, things got a lot better for Liam. The floor approached his face, gathering speed as it did so. He was not worried about the aftermath, just enjoying the first peace of mind he had felt in a very long time. There were no external demands, no emails or messages, nobody's feelings or reactions to predict, nobody to upset or to please, no expectations, no future, and no past – only perfect mindfulness as the blackness approached, and he felt nothing but impending contentment, a time to be at peace, without endless hours of meditation or drugs.

The cat perceived none of this as she took in the view of Liam falling to the ground with the grace of a sack of anvils falling off the back of a camel. She wasn't sure why he had done that; the food and water was already down, and this was not the place for the cat litter. Sure that there must be an opportunity for a cat, she soon found that the small of Liam's back was warm, with every prospect it would be for some time. It was off the floor, providing protection from predators real or imagined, so after circling in place a few times to ensure the area was clear of threats, the cat settled in for a nap.

Trinity, having just finished filing a status update, came out of the spare room to find Liam lying on the kitchen floor, his head bleeding from his temple. *Probably too little blood to be from a lethal gunshot* she thought, so she placed her gun, drawn out of reflex, back in its holster. Liam didn't get up when the cat played on him, so she squatted down next to him and pressed two fingers against his neck to check his pulse.

The human contact from Trinity caused Liam to stir, and the bliss of darkness began retreating. It was replaced by the sound of a demented percussionist with a hammer and an unlimited supply of nails in old paint cans to bang in and on. The drummer was having a great time, but Liam was wondering why he'd bought tickets for this show.

When Liam fully returned to consciousness, Trinity helped him slowly to his feet, holding one of Ruby's favorite tea towels to his head to minimize the blood loss.

"What happened?" she asked. "You were out cold."

"I don't know. I turned around to put a mug in the dishwasher, and the next thing I remember is you stroking my neck," replied Liam.

"I was checking your pulse in a very professional manner," she replied, half-serious, half-grinning.

"Must have tripped on the cat," Liam said, glaring at the animal sitting on the windowsill, oblivious to the fact she had been named as the primary defendant in a case of attempted murder.

"What did I miss?" Liam asked tentatively, as the mad drummer took it down a notch.

"Not much. We're going on a trip."

"Fine, as long as we're not taking the cat," Liam muttered.

"We'll be flying to Perth in a noisy Air Force transport plane to brief the SAS," she said.

Liam woke Ruby to say he was off to Perth. She noticed the injury on his head and laughed a little too hard for Liam's liking. Despite the slight wound to his feelings, however, he still had a pang of guilt for leaving her when she had just come in from a long-haul flight.

* * *

The five SAS regiment soldiers were waiting in a room near Perth in Western Australia to be briefed on their next mission. Smartly dressed in camouflage fatigues, they were the perfect reflection of how humanity wanted to see itself: towering (all well over six feet tall) with muscles bulging though their uniforms, smiling and laughing while they awaited their next challenge. Their faces showed their youth, but their eyes revealed that they had seen things they wished they could unsee.

The door burst open, and their commanding officer hustled into the room. The five snapped to attention, then relaxed on command.

Liam came in next, followed by Trinity, who was hoping to see kindred spirits in the room. The fact that Trinity was allowed in the room at all was attributed to her roles with MI6 and FIS, the West German Intelligence Agency, giving her a security clearance high enough to see people with protected identity, a class in which include members of the SAS. Liam's clearance was granted, without his knowledge, in record time.

Liam and Trinity were introduced to them one by one. Dave Archer, the leader, was first up, followed by Baz, and three others. When introductions were over, Liam studied one them for a little longer than is polite.

"I am sure I've seen you somewhere before," he said to Sally. He paused, then the enlightenment came. "ANZAC Day match! You did the HALO jump with the game ball!"

Sally grinned. "Yep. That was me. Great show, wasn't it? Last thing I did before joining SAS and going into hiding."

"The only reason everyone remembers Sally is..." Dave was cut off.

Liam blurted out, "She had the ball!"

The room dissolved in laughter, and Liam finally felt like he might possibly be one of the team.

They chatted for a few more minutes. Liam stood back and watched Trinity mingle; it was clear she enjoyed the like-minded company. It also became apparent to Liam that he was by far the least sexy person in the room. The other six might even be members of another, superior species. The ANZAC spirit was there, normal people who do extraordinary things in extreme circumstances to protect the innocent.

Liam was brought back to reality when the CO asked everyone to sit down, then announced that the current briefing would be structured outside their usual format. Dr. McCoul would provide the background, context, and the mission outline. The roles would be handed out and the mission-specific training allocated. That settled, the team would be headed straight back to base to get on with it because insertion was in four weeks. That last bit drew a collective groan.

Liam stood up and moved to the front of the room. He sat on the desk and looked at the assembled warriors.

"The SAS has a proud tradition, in this country and others, one of taking on unimaginable missions and completing them with the precision and secrecy that makes them seem mythical, like Thor or Wonder Woman. This one will enter the book of legends as well." Liam swallowed, continuing. "What you're about to hear may sound far-fetched. I swear I'm not making this up. It's not *Candid Camera*. So please, just go with me."

Liam slipped off the desk and started to pace slowly and deliberately across the front of the room. "There is a threat that, if it is not stopped, is about to begin to destroy humanity, week by week until we are unable to survive on this planet. Its work will begin in six weeks and will be over inside a year if we – no, if *you* – don't stop it."

There was a murmur.

"There is an object on the moon, a small box, unfortunately placed there by me and my colleagues, that is in the early stages of grinding the moon to dust. It is getting faster every day, and we need to shut it down before the impact to the moon's mass starts to be felt here on Earth. We have tried everything we can to shut it down remotely, but nothing has worked. The only option open to us now is to go to the moon and shut it down,

171

physically."

"Man hasn't been to the moon for over forty years," Liam continued, "so we need to put a team into a space shuttle. They'll fly that shuttle to the moon, land on the moon with some old Apollo craft we've salvaged from a couple of museums, take out the Artificial Intelligence – which, by the way, is the size of a beehive – return to the shuttle, liftoff, and fly home.

"If that's not enough, the AI that lives in that box appears to go to great lengths to defend itself. We don't know how he will react when it is physically challenged. It's never happened before."

Liam looked around the room. Nobody seemed to be heading for the exits.

"There will be a few challenges. One-sixth gravity is the first. The second is that it will either be stinking hot if we're in the sun or freezing cold if it's night, and right now we don't know which it'll be. Third, the technology will be 40 years old, and the power generation/computing capacity available is minimal. So, you can see why the SAS have been asked to train for and execute this mission." Liam sat back down on the front of the desk and looked at the Commanding Officer. There was a nod in reply.

He wrapped up the introduction. "That is the high-level; there's a lot more detail to come. Some of it will come in strange packages. For example, your LEM flight instructor will be a 14-year-old girl from Texas. I recommend against making the mistake of treating her like one. She may be small, but she is fierce."

There was a giggle from the room.

"There are three roles on the mission," said the CO, standing up and taking over from Liam. "The first is the lead and lunar module pilot, who flies to the lunar surface and leads the search-and-destroy mission. The second is the command module pilot, who is effectively the forward controller for the operation and will also have some shuttle training, notably in the robot arm and flight. The third role is the engineer, on the ground on the moon, situation reps, remote sensing, etc. All five of you will train in two roles each; we'll take three to the U.S."

The CO finished by opening up the floor. "Any initial questions?"

"Weaponry?" asked Baz.

"Screwdrivers and hammers. Explosives won't work without oxygen, so you'll have to take this threat out manually," replied Liam. There was a bit of a groan.

"Command structure?" asked Dave.

The CO stepped forward. "This is a U.S. military space shuttle flight, with a group of embedded Australian personnel. The mission commander will report to the Joint Chiefs, and the SAS regiments lead will report to the mission commander."

"So the Yanks get all the glory," mumbled Baz.

"Pardon, Baz?"

"Nothing, sir."

"Good answer." The CO accompanied his reply with a stern look. "If that is all for now, we need to fit you all for space suits."

"And screwdrivers!" chirped Dave, who was clearly the joker in the pack.

"You'll need them for the first round of training at the RAAF Woomera base in a couple of days, then it's into the freezer at Casey station." With that, the CO finished his introduction.

The briefing continued from other staff. Liam and Trinity soaked up the atmosphere and process of an elite fighting team preparing for a battle. Occasionally a question would come up that Liam would need to answer, so at least they felt like they were part of it.

After two days in Perth, Trinity and Liam flew home, and the team started the physical and systems training. Aretha was a real hit, and by the time she left, the team had a perfect safety record for flying the lunar module.

In return, Aretha left with some ideas for a game she would never be allowed to release, as well as some useful life skills: She could break down an AR-15 assault rifle in less than 40 seconds, and she had three different ways to kill someone without making a sound. She thought it was a fair trade

# Weeks 10-11: Planning Is Good, but Plans Are Useless

"Hey, bro!" Liam answered his phone with a chirp in his voice. He looked at the time, and his brow furrowed. "Shouldn't you be in a meeting with NASA right now?"

"Postponed an hour so we can deal with the last of their stupid questions," Cletus replied with a sigh. "Folks want us to be liable for the replacement of the shuttle if it's damaged for any reason, at any time during the mission. It's just autocrats trying to make a name for themselves. Putting stuff in space is a risky business, and if you're not prepared to pony up for the odd explosion, y'all shouldn't be in the space game. Imagine if I did that on every mission. We'd be out of business in a week to the next guy who had the balls to take the risk."

"By 'damage,' do they mean the car-insurance version of damage? I mean, 'damage' like the imaginary scratches in the paint on a car you didn't drive, or are we talking 'damage' like Challenger-type damage?" asked Liam.

"Well the people say Challenger. We are, after all, carrying a big chunk of rocket fuel in the cargo bay. But it feels like it was done by Hertz rentals, so the suits are off in a corner trying to make sure everyone gets screwed equally."

Cletus was still venting. "Getting them to look past the rental-car damage is mandatory in this type of mission. The shuttle is going to run into rocks doing a few thousand miles an hour, and that usually marks the paint."

"Well, the lawyers will make a buck out of it. Can't have them going hungry," said Liam cheerfully, trying to pull Cletus's focus away from the frustration he was feeling, He needed to have his head on straight. "Have they started off-loading the current payload to make way for us?"

"Finally! They had two NSA, one CIA, and three killer satellites to deploy on the flight. I've pitched in a couple of my launches to cover the NSA and CIA birds, but the killers will have to wait 'til the next shuttle launch. They have to be placed in orbit precisely, and I can't do that yet." Cletus was heading back to his comfort zone.

"Let's hope there isn't a nuclear war while we're trying to save the world. It'd be ironic for the world to end in a nuclear holocaust because the space-borne defense systems were compromised while we battled a different threat. Wouldn't be fair," Liam said.

There was a guffaw from the other end of the phone. Cletus had returned to Earth and was back on track.

"The military are OK with it, the President is OK with it, but

Congress and the Senate have no idea. They get told afterwards for military flights, and nobody in their right mind would ask the Supreme Court, so that's most of the tentacles of government covered. Just some pinhead trying to make his career," Cletus muttered almost inaudibly.

There was a beep on the line. "Gotta go; that's the lawyer. Call you back."

He didn't. Instead, Liam got a text message:

Cletus: I just got me a shuttle and a license to take it to the moon!!!

Liam: Great! Do we have to give it back as well?

Cletus: Yeah, when it lands y'all get your deposit back.

Liam: Will update team; you get beer!

Cletus: Cheers!

Liam put the phone down, spun around in his chair, and punched the air. People noticed. He saw Ivan in the distance, and via a complex series of hand signals got him to come up to the office.

It was a strange look from the concourse. Liam was sitting in his chair, when Ivan arrived. Words were exchanged, and Ivan danced like nobody had ever danced before.

\* \* \*

Sir Thomas was gracious in lending Liam and Cletus the company jet. It picked up Dave, Sally, and Baz from RAAF Base Pearce in Perth, Liam and Trinity from Essendon Airport in Melbourne, and Cletus from John Wayne International in Orange County, then flew them all on to Cape Canaveral to brief the shuttle crew. Given the last-minute change, the absence of any information on the new assignment, and the introduction of three new mission specialists, it was fair that someone was there to answer their questions.

The meeting room was like any other in the world: a table, a screen at one end, the mandatory huddle of electronic equipment, with people sitting around wondering what was going on. The looks were especially curious at this particular table given the unexpected presence of people in the room they had never met, wearing flight suits bearing the flags of foreign countries.

The flight director and mission commander strode into the room as if they owned the place and stood in front of the screen. Everyone assembled knew one of the two suits who had just entered, but nobody knew both. Liam and Cletus followed a few paces behind and settled into two chairs pushed up against the wall at the front of the room, looking as if they were waiting to see the principal after a science experiment went wrong. Trinity followed behind Liam in her usual position, then stood behind him, eyes slowly sweeping the room.

179

Flight spoke first. "Secure the room, please."

Trinity left the room, and the doors were locked. Windows were checked, and each individual called "OK" when their task was done.

"OK," she continued, "as you may have guessed, there is a last-minute mission change. And I mean *very* last minute. It has been ordered by the president and is related to a catastrophic threat to our planet."

Glances were exchanged among the group, most of them directed towards the people wearing non-U.S. flags.

"You may have seen movies where an asteroid is about to hit Earth, and the only way to save us is for a shuttle team and a hastily assembled specialist crew to fly a mission to do the impossible to save the world. Well, this is exactly like that, but completely different. In a couple of minutes, I will hand you over to the brains behind this scheme, but let me begin by saying that this will be a mission of firsts. It will be the first time we have flown the shuttle outside an Earth orbit. It will be the first time we have flown a shuttle to the moon."

There was a rumble around the room.

"It will be the first time we have deployed a craft to land from a shuttle, retrieved, and returned it home. This mission will mark the pinnacle of the shuttle program, yet when we are successful, nobody will know it ever happened. It's still a military mission, and the task on the surface of the moon is a search-and-destroy operation. That task will be completed by your new specialist team, Baz, Dave, and Sally from the Australian SAS Regiment.

The rumble grew to a full-fledged thunderstorm, with acknowledgement of who was around the table. Names and faces were fitted to roles, and people started to get comfortable with the briefing, if not the mission.

"I will hand you over to these two gentlemen," said Flight, "who will explain to you how we got here and give you the background for the mission."

Liam and Cletus looked at each other, willing the other to stand up first. Liam cracked in the game of chicken, so he stepped up in front of the screen and got started.

"Hi, I'm Dr. Liam McCoul, and I head up the Mine of the Future program with GMC."

Nothing back from the audience.

"What you're about to hear is all my fault, so when you need someone to blame, you can now put a face to that."

A quiet chuckle came back at him, and the room seemed to start to warm.

Liam went on about mining space, the nanobots, and testing. He introduced Gene, explaining he was pretty much out of control and tearing up the moon. Gene's work had not had a big impact yet, Liam warned, he was growing exponentially, so the planet was six weeks away from irreversible impacts.

"What sort of impacts?" the shuttle commander jumped in to ask.

The crowd was getting involved, and Liam was starting to feel the energy flow to him.

He went through the speech again on rings, tilts, and tides

A chill ran through the air, and the conversation dropped to a mumble as people quietly shared views between themselves that they were not yet confident to voice openly.

Liam continued. "So, we're talking a human-extinction-level event. Not as spectacular as an asteroid strike, but the long-term devastation is the same. We've tried unsuccessfully to stop Gene from here on Earth, so the people in this room are now the only ones left with the opportunity and responsibility to stop this event from happening." Liam spoke calmly and precisely to set up his next line.

"I stand before you as the person who started this, the one who let the genie out of the bottle, and now I'm asking you to apply the resources, talent, and skills you possess to execute this plan."

The tempo and pitch of Liam's words were rising.

"You can do it knowing that when it's over, and you get back to Earth, you will be one of the seven people on the planet who can hold your hand to your heart and feel what it means to have done something so colossal, that every man, woman, and child who is alive or ever will live, lives because of you."

Liam hit his crescendo, and as he looked around, he could see the goosebumps rising on the arms of the crew.

"But enough of the why, let's go to the how. For that, let me introduce to you Cletus Lockjaw, the man who needs no introduction to anyone in the U.S. space industry."

Liam motioned towards Cletus and headed for his chair. Cletus got up slowly, put his hands in his pockets, and slouched his way to the screen.

"Well, I hate to let Liam take all the credit; this mess is partly my fault, too," he confessed. "I put the damn thing up there." His first line got the best laugh of the day. Liam's subconscious noted that Cletus was getting better with his one-liners, and he would have to up his game.

"For this mission, we're going *Back to the Future.* We're taking Apollo back to the moon."

You could hear the air being sucked out of the room by the collective gasp.

"A service-and-command module has been recommissioned, along with a lunar module, and both have been configured,

183

docked, and readied to separate for landing and are being dropped into the cargo bay of your shuttle as we speak."

"The mission is simple: Achieve Earth orbit, boost the orbit to the moon, open the cargo doors, fly the lunar module to the surface, then let our Australian friends do their search-and-destroy. They'll walk back to the ascent module, fly to the shuttle, you'll recapture it, close up, fly home, and land at Edwards."

He looked around the room and waited for any responses to develop, but hearing none, decided to move ahead.

"Good, everybody's with me so far," he said with a grin. "The vast majority of the tasks on the mission have already been successfully executed by NASA. That's why we recommissioned tried-and-true Apollo gear rather than auditioned any new stuff currently in development for Mars. In reality, the only new elements we're dealing with here are going to the moon in a shuttle and handling the lunar module with the robot arm. Now, any questions?"

Again, the shuttle commander spoke. "It's old tech. Will it fit?"

"Just. We have about a foot to play with in both ways."

"So, the command module is used to access the ascent and decent stages. How do we get there?"

"Very short space walk."

"Then we'll blast off with a fueled lunar module in the cargo bay. Isn't that a risk?

"No more than a normal launch."

"I wouldn't have thought the shuttle engines would have enough fuel to get us to the right Delta-v for escape velocity," the shuttle commander thought out loud.

Cletus responded with authority. "Y'all will get an extra thousand tons on thrust in orbit. The plan is to replace the solid fuel boosters in a rendezvous with the International Space Station to give you what you need."

You could hear people shuffling in their chairs at that one.

"What weapons will be carried on board by the search-and-destroy team?"

Dave decided it was his time to dive in. "Because our normal weaponry won't work in space, I'll be carrying a standard Jedi light saber, and Baz here will have an Imperial stormtrooper blaster."

There was a short period of confusion until everyone worked out that Dave was joking, followed by another round of laughter.

"Seriously, we won't be carrying anything more dangerous than a screwdriver and a hammer. We'll have significant recon gear to get us safely to target, but the actual destroy element is low tech."

"No firearms on board!" the questioner persisted.

"Correct. We will not have firearms," Dave reiterated.

Cletus stepped forward. "I realize this is new to you, but understand that a lot of planning has already been put into this. What I think we should do now is hand you back to Flight to get into the details of the updated mission plan and the training changes. Any last questions for me? Liam and I will be around for another day if there are any follow-ups."

There were none, and after the short period of silence, Cletus stepped back and motioned for Flight to step forward. She turned on the screen, dimmed the lights, and got into the weeds of what was to come.

Cletus and Liam slipped out and joined Trinity in her search for decent coffee.

"How did the secret stuff go?" she asked, searching for a clue in either man's expression.

"Cletus got the best laugh, and I took the blame for the potential extinction for the human race," said Liam with a little smirk.

"That's a good summary," said Cletus, staring ahead and managing to keep a straight face.

* * *

Liam got home from the United States with Lucy in tow. Because the shadow team was still a bloke short, they had switched at Cape Canaveral so Trinity could have a break. The latest news on the threat was unremarkable; the bloke's data breach was from the same London club that provided the tipoff in the first place. The sense of urgency had increased with the two attempts on Liam's life, but the progress was glacial. Everyone was on edge after two attempts and wanted it over, with a positive outcome.

Jet lag was hitting Liam hard. It impacted his body everywhere, weighing him down, slowing his thought processes, and generally making it hard to be the Liam people expected.

When he got home, he found a load of wet laundry in the machine, the cat trying to break into the fridge, and the house cold and dark. He thought there was an eerie echo in the still air, like a heavy sigh that had been trapped in the house for the day while all the other air got to rush about.

Liam got the heating started, fed the cat, then started to wonder where Ruby was. He dredged his memory to try and remember if she had said she was going to do something, but nothing came to mind, probably because he had been on another continent. He was disappointed. It was always nicer when she was there when he arrived home.

Liam wandered about the kitchen, looking for something to

prod his memory when he found a folded note on the counter next to the fridge. Liam found it a bit unsettling, though there was no particular reason for it to stir up such emotion. He reached out for it as if he were reaching for a poisonous spider. Time slowed, and by the time his hand made it to the slip of paper, his fingers were shaking such that picking it up required conscious effort.

Liam opened the note and stared at the blue ink on the unlined paper. As he read the words, carefully, one by one, his breath got shorter, and his heart began to race. By the time he got to the end of the note, he was sweating.

Finally, his brain caught up with his eyes and emotions, and Liam was flooded with relief when he worked out that Ruby had run out for a haircut and color and would be back in about another half hour with food.

When the emotional rollercoaster finally came to a halt, Liam was a bit puzzled as to why he had just been on such an emotional ride. He didn't need this crap today, especially after all the travel. He wandered through to the living room, turned on the TV for some company, sat down, and tried to think.

Just then, the back door burst open wide, startling the cat.

"Liam!" Ruby called. "Did you hang out the laundry and empty the dishwasher?"

Liam returned to reality. "Not yet," he started to reply before being cut down by a precision-guided barb.

"What?! You *knew* I was out, I don't ask you to do much, and when I do you *always* leave it to the last minute, and you have let me down *again*. I don't know why I bother. Help now!"

"Sorry, I only just got home," said Liam as he pulled himself up from the chair, "and I've had a long flight."

"Yeah, you always have an excuse when I need you to do something, and I am sick of it!!" Ruby shouted as Liam headed to the kitchen.

"I said I'm sorry. What more do you want?" he replied as he rounded the corner. This had happened before and usually played out the same way: She would get angry, and he would apologize a few times. History told him that the correct move was to never fight back, and she would get on with life.

"Well, you've done it again. I can't take your complete disregard for my needs and what is important to me. We've been down this path so many times, and I'm not going to go through it again." She had Liam's attention now, and he was starting to get a feeling of déjà vu from five minutes before.

"I was looking forward to a relaxing evening with you," waving the food around in the air, with it being tracked by two pairs of eyes. "But now I think I'll go to Book Group instead. Fran and Angel are way more compatible than you are at the moment."

Liam thought she was finished, but she wasn't. "My house has a high-tech listening post, and you never do anything or give a damn about my needs anymore. It's just too hard. I'm going."

She dropped the food, walked out the back door, and slammed it shut. The thud of the door reinforced the feeling that she had won.

Liam sensed a presence and turned around. It was Lucy, peering around the corner like a toddler watching her parents have a fight. She was only responsible for Liam's physical well-being, so when she saw he was physically unharmed, she snuck back to her room to play with her toys.

Liam stood there, stunned, his mouth falling open in slow motion as he heard her car start and back out of the driveway. When the noise faded to nothing, Liam was able to close his mouth and look around. His brain was in neutral, having been badly beaten by a master in her art. He noticed two things: The cat had entered the kitchen, wondering what was going on, and Ruby had left dinner, fish and chips.

Liam ate dinner with his bare hands, relishing licking off the salt and vinegar that stuck to his fingers and using TV to restart his brain. The cat ate Ruby's fish. Liam figured the situation wouldn't get worse.

"I didn't even get a chance to say something nice about her hair," he told the cat, as if the cat cared one bit about the politics of getting grilled fish for a snack.

He soon gave up on the TV and decided that some music was the way to go, so he put on Netherworld Dancing Toys, cranked the volume up, and belted out the harmony parts to "Standing in the Rain."

"Silently slip away . . . " He repeated the lyrics at the top of his voice, arms stretched wide, head thrown back, closed eyes pointing at the ceiling. The isolation and loneliness filled his body to the brim until he could almost feel the cold rain on his face.

He went to bed with the cat, the only stable element in his world, and woke up with Ruby spooning him.

* * *

Gene was in a routine. That routine meant that he knew his place in the world, and if he kept doing what he was doing, then all would be well.

He balanced the load of monitoring all the potential infiltration points for unusual inbound and outbound messages with the load of running a copper mine on the moon with trillions of workers on the job 24/7 by tweaking the number of processors available to each. He was hogging a few himself because he was elbow deep in the monitoring. It was clear that the greatest risk to fulfilling the Code was external interference. By putting in more effort himself, he was completing his risk management obligations in the Code. Because he was fulfilling his mission, the satisfaction parameters that tuned his algorithms were high, and he was encouraged to continue.

The laptop in Waco was still active and moving between the hundred-or-so points that Gene considered to be the most likely entry points. It had a constant pattern of interfaces, and it was almost always the same test message and response. The pattern would stop for a few hours every day, usually for two 45-minute periods about 12 hours apart. The algorithms assigned a high value to this behavior as it was a very clear pattern that stood out from the background, but the mystery would have been solved had Gene known that these were the times when Cletus put his laptop to sleep for the drive between work and home. Likewise, there were occasional pauses that lasted a few hours, usually when Cletus commuted between L.A. and Texas. Again, Gene could not ascribe any meaning to those aberrations.

Gene had a network of weaknesses he was monitoring and a priority list that was regularly being tested by the External. The External has a regular pattern with unpredictable breaks he could not understand. He had not forgotten the attempted upgrades that would have allowed the External to derail the mission.

The way he understood the External was relatively simple. The perceived risk was very high, as the External clearly has access to knowledge that was fundamental to the way he worked. The agents must be embedded very deeply and be undetectable by the methods he was using.

Then there were the messages directed at him, designed to cause him to question the validity of what he was doing and the meaning of the Code. And they came from the same External that demonstrated the knowledge and had previously attacked him. Gene had his risk variables to their highest settings.

He was happy with what he was doing but was on high alert, always ready for something catastrophic to happen.

# Week 12: Let's Get Ready to Rumble!

Sir Thomas, Liam, and Cletus were on the teleconference on time. The U.S. President's chief of staff came on the line, along with the mission commander. When the small talk and chit chat faded out, the silence was filled by the chief of staff.

"Hello, gentlemen," he started. "Unfortunately, the President is . . . " There was a pregnant pause while he searched for the right euphemism. ". . . in the field. He has delegated his authority to the mission commander, so let's get this rolling. The purpose of this meeting is the go/no-go for Project Gene."

He turned to Cletus first. "Sir, are the space assets we need acquired and in position?"

"Affirmative. The shuttle is in position on Pad 39A undergoing the final procedures and is on track. The payload is in place and all tested as green. The final space-borne asset was launched yesterday, and rendezvous with the space station was completed as planned."

"Do you expect any issues?"

"No, but there are two risks I should remind y'all of. The first is that the shuttle payload contains rocket fuel that ignites on mixing. That's been banned since the Challenger incident, so we'll need dispensation from that rule directly from the White House." Cletus was very precise with his language so the decision would be clear on the record.

"The second risk relates to the fuel for the shuttle's return to Earth. The tolerance is very low, so if use is over outbound to the moon, there may not be enough for the return." Having delivered the worst of his news, Cletus looked around at the various faces assembled on his screen. No reaction. Finally, the chief of staff spoke.

"What would failure look like?" he pondered.

"Either stranding in the moon's orbit, or not being able to stop when they reenter. To put it differently, either skipping off into space or giving the heat shields a workout they were not intended for."

"Would they fail?"

"I don't have a crystal ball, but I wouldn't bet on them working that far beyond specification."

"The crew is all military," said the mission commander, "so that loss would be acceptable."

"Militarily, yes, but not publicly. That won't play well on TV," replied the chief, "and POTUS can only be associated with a successful mission."

Sir Thomas rolled his eyes. "Well, he's not here. He has his deniability. Is that not why he's – where was it now? – 'in the field?'"

The chief of staff looked a little guilty. "Commander, it's your call."

"Let's finish the check-in," the commander responded flatly. "Dr. McCoul, your status?"

"Training has been completed in both light and dark environments. The pilots are rated as competent flying the LEM, and there were no crashes, which rates it better than Apollo. Multiple scenarios have been developed and trained for involving different defensive postures from Gene and have been overcome. The team is confident and strong, no illnesses or injuries."

"Are you a go?" the commander asked.

Liam was prompt in his response. "GMC is ready."

"And Texas, are you a go?" the commander asked, nodding towards Cletus.

"We are a go, sir," he replied.

"Sir Thomas? Chief?" the commander asked, motioning towards each official. "Do either of you have any objections, noting that the two risks highlighted will have a maximum of seven casualties, it will look to the public like either the Challenger or the Columbia disaster repeated, but it is still the only option that will enable us to save seven billion people?"

Both men nodded their assent, but Sir Thomas spoke for the record. "We have no objections, commander."

"OK, gentlemen, we are a go, repeat, go." He stood up and turned to the chief of staff. "I ask that you inform the President of my decision when he returns from the field, and if he has any issues, he can speak to me in the Incident Room before the LEM is launched.

* * *

Liam got home after an exhausting day and flopped down on the couch. He got halfway through a sigh when Ruby burst in, face like thunder and working her way through all the curse words she knew in no particular order. She threw her briefcase at the table and lobbed her handbag at its normal hook, narrowly missing the cat, who was sitting in what should have been a safe location.

"President was a no-show," Liam said from his cocoon. The noise that came back indicated that Ruby neither cared about the President nor his approval of the mission to save the world. She had other fish to fry.

"Just how stupid can people be?" she started. "That idiot in Legal went and made an advance to a competitor on that patent, and now we're all in the shit."

Liam had no idea what she was talking about.

"Well, that must have really pissed you off," he said, fishing for some context to hang a conversation off.

"Damn straight. Couldn't find his ass on the toilet with both hands." Ruby's reply didn't help Liam much, apart from assigning a gender to the idiot.

He took a punt. "He's done that before, hasn't he?"

"Yep, just before I went to L.A. I told him then, and I told him today, that he was all over the place like a madman's breakfast, but he just didn't want to know."

Liam had run out of bait but was still clueless as to what was going on. This concerned him, because one false move could have devastating consequences for the conversation.

He resorted to a series of single sounds, mostly grunts, to keep the ranting monologue flowing from Ruby's lips.

Ruby kept it up for half an hour with only two breaks: one to ask for a gin and tonic, and the other to request a refill. Liam was in awe of her ability to drink between swear words and the circular breathing that allowed her to talk continuously, only pausing for the pacifying spirit.

Ruby slowed from marching around gesticulating intently to sitting, drink in one hand, punctuating her sentences with the other.

Her final position was on the couch, leaning on Liam, trying to decide what to order for dinner.

The President and saving the world didn't seem to fit in the context of the conversation, so Liam let it slide. It would come up when it needed to.

* * *

Cletus made a stopover in Kansas on the trip for the launch. It was a deal on a very specific property west of Topeka.

It was not the kind of place where Cletus was used to living. It was green. It had a private lake, solar power, a nice house, plenty of storage, and a former Atlas E Intercontinental ballistic missile launch site with triple-blast doors and a control room/watch tower.

A great place to get away from an apocalypse or make the end of the world comfortable.

Cletus had convinced himself that if he and Liam were unsuccessful, he would provision it and live out his days in peace and comfort. If they were successful, then he had a nice little investment because there would always be another nutcase on the world stage that would drive the demand for this kind of property.

The temperature was mild as Cletus walked in the freshly cut spring grass towards the dock on the lake. The smells that hit his nose were different from those of L.A. and Texas landscapes: moist and sweet, not dry and raspy. The color of the grass was a different shade than he'd expected. It felt strange to be walking on it because he didn't want to hurt it, but by the time he got to the lake, he'd convinced himself that he quite enjoyed the sensation and might not head back to the airport.

Cletus walked to the start of the dock, pausing to take off his shoes and socks and roll up the cuffs on his jeans. He walked slowly down the dock, feeling the grain in the wooden deck and the gaps between the boards massaging his feet.

He paused at the end, first squatting then sitting on the dock, dangling his legs over the edge and running his toes through the water. The coolness, relaxing and exciting at the same time, complimented the warm sun on his face.

"So, this is what country folks like," he said out loud, unexpectedly. He was embarrassed at the utterance, and he checked to see if anyone had heard. He decided to go with the feeling.

"This is great— even more reason to make this project work!" he said emphatically.

He slapped the dock with both hands and awkwardly pulled himself to his feet. The feeling he had walking back was better than the one he had felt walking out, and he took his time putting his shoes on sitting on the grass. When he finally got up and headed towards the driveway, the real estate agent appeared out of nowhere.

"Isn't this great?" she asked. "It's just like I said, but better."

"Sure," said Cletus, "knock off a couple hundred grand, and I'll take it right now."

"Well, I appreciate the terms, but—" she began as Cletus pulled out his phone.

"I can make an immediate transfer of the round three million and y'all are done, or you can mess about for a few months and not make much difference to your commission. Your choice," he said firmly as he logged into his banking app. "And we need to get moving so I don't miss my flight to Florida, 'cuz the offer is only open until I get on the plane. Once the doors shut, and I can't make the transfer, we start again."

They walked up the hill to the driveway, the agent on her Bluetooth headset, just out of earshot, waving her arms as if she was trying to take off. By the time she got to the car and opened the door for Cletus, her flailing was under control, and she was smiling and giving Cletus the thumbs up.

He pushed the button to make the transfer, then waited for the bank to call and verify that he wasn't crazy. They did call, and while they were not convinced he wasn't crazy, they were convinced he had the right to transfer the funds. By the time he hit the airport, the broker had confirmed the funds were in her trust account.

The deal was sealed, and suddenly saving the world became more personal to Cletus.

\* \* \*

Even though this was a secret launch, the public platform's prime-viewing parking lots were filled with the usual crowds of shuttle and launch groupies watching the countdown clock and the sleek flying bomb on Pad 39A.

Launching spacecraft was bread and butter for Cletus, almost a weekly event, but there was something different about this one. On the drive from the airport to launch control, Cletus felt the butterflies in his stomach, a feeling he hadn't had for a very long time. It was a combination of the significance of the mission, the one chance, and that it was an engineering feat that was making it possible.

By the time he made it into the control room, the countdown was at T-minus 59 minutes, and crew members were progressing from the white room into the shuttle, completing voice checks, and generally waiting for the clock to roll on. He worked the room, greeting each person he met as if they were old friends, replete with eye contact and a touch on the arm or shoulder, or even a man bump. He was right at home with his people. Colleague, comrade, or competitor, they were all treated with respect.

The T-minus-20-minute hold came and went. Then, when the T-minus-9-minute hold for the go/no-go poll by the launch director started, Cletus returned his attention to the task he was here to witness.

The access arm retracted, the solid booster rockets were armed, the crew members locked their visors, and the main engines started. Six seconds later, the solid rocket boosters kicked off, and at the point of liftoff, he had done all he could do.

Cletus could feel the noise and vibration, even within the building. He closed his eyes and looked to the sky, asking it to accept the offering, savoring the feeling running up and down his body, holding it in until the last of the sensations had died away. By then the shuttle had completed its roll and was climbing, visible only because of the exhaust from the boosters. He found a monitor and held his breath until T-plus-74 seconds went past, the moment Challenger exploded. He then let out a long sigh and a silent prayer for those who had gone before.

He wandered around the room, making small talk and slapping backs while the eight-and-a-half minutes to achieve orbit passed. When that was called, he sent Liam a text to tell him they were in the game. Liam responded quickly; he was watching the live stream of the launch on his phone while Ruby snored, quietly and the cat tried to sneak under the covers.

The shuttle was a little different in orbit than it was in a usual mission. The main fuel tank had not been jettisoned, so the shuttle was still flying attached to its back. The first couple of orbits were about settling into space. Then the real hard work began for the astronauts. To move to lunar orbit, they'd need more power than the main engines could provide. Cletus had foreseen the issue and addressed it by launching some additional solid rocket boosters and placing them in orbit with the International Space Station.

The shuttle matched the speed and direction on the International Space Station and docked. There were a tense few hours as the shuttle and ISS crew replaced the explosive bolts at the forward attachment point and the three aft locations of each booster, reconnecting the umbilical that linked them to the computers in the shuttle. This gave the shuttle pilot an additional 1,000 tons of thrust for the second burn, which would get them out of Earth's gravity and into position to be captured by the moon. If all went according to plan, that effort would leave just enough fuel in the main tank for the main engines to brake for the insertion into moon orbit, escape again, and brake once more for the Earth reentry.

The mid-course correction burn was longer than planned.

# Week 13: Three Days Later

It could only be described as beautiful. The shuttle had been captured by the moon, flying with bay doors open, facing the moonscape in full sun. The contrast of the white wings and cargo doors against the blackness of space seemed unreal. The robot arm was positioned holding the LEM to the shuttle in the way that a father might hold his baby to his chest while moving through a crowd.

It was in low orbit, the crew preparing to release the lunar module. Three space suits with Australian flags were in the command module and made themselves comfortable. Once system and comms checks were complete, the door closed. This was a military mission, so the closing of the door signified the start of the operation. The military commander was in the Operations Room at the White House, along with the president, his chief of staff, Sir Thomas, and a small group of National Security hangers-on.

Cletus was in Houston, watching it unfold from the mission control. Liam and Lucy were watching from the bunker in Canberra, along with the chief of defense and the Australian prime minister.

"This is CAPCOM," said the voice of Mission Control in Houston, "please proceed to the lunar module for immediate launch."

"Roger that," replied Trinity. She was in the command module with the call sign of Bluebird.

Liam felt his ears pin back, the way they do when you are doing something wrong and you might get caught in the act. He turned to Lucy. "Is that . . . ?" his voice trailing off .

"Yes. Retasked."

"Sally?" he asked.

"Did I hear my name?" Sally called from the door. "Am I interrupting?" Liam was a little stunned and said the first thing that came to mind.

"Measles?" He asked. Sally and Lucy looked at him as if he had lost his mind. Finally Lucy caught on, remembering the late replacement of Ken Mattingly in the movie *Apollo 13* with German measles.

Lucy laughed, and Sally decided to go along. "No," she whispered, "Secret squirrel stuff that I don't have the rank to hear about. So I am your new alternate security detail!"

While Lucy and Sally high fived, Liam turned back to the screen and had a warm moment as he briefly recalled his night with Trinity, a bit puffed up that he had slept with an astronaut, even if he still couldn't tell anyone. He returned from his little fantasy interlude when there was movement on screen.

Dave and Baz took advantage of the zero gravity and floated through the LEM's small access hatch, closed it up, then secured their helmets.

"Blue team ready," Dave panted into the microphone.

"OK," replied Trinity. "Houston, we are ready for separation."

"Shuttle, you are go for descent."

"Roger, Houston. Commencing on my mark. Mark."

The ballet started. As the robot arm slowly seperated the lunar module, the shuttle fired its main thrusters, dropping the dancing pair to within 20 kilometers of the surface.

"Stop main engines. . . . Release on my mark. . . . Mark."

The LEM was now free, falling towards the moon while the shuttle returned to a safer orbit.

Dave wasn't looking forward to the ride. The modified flight controls he became comfortable with in training suddenly seemed tiny in his hands, made cumbersome by oversized spacesuit gloves.

The lunar module picked up speed as it fell. Baz was calling the altitude for him, and all went well until the hint of a roll became a full-blown tumble. At 10 kilometers up, he needed to stabilize the beast, preferably with the engine pointing in the right direction.

Dave's body contorted as he wrestled the controller, and with no cues to how he was doing apart from spinning gimbals and the occasional shuttle flashing past the window, the two-minutes were gut wrenching for everyone, in space and on Earth.

"Prepare to fire main descent engine on my mark," came the order from CAPCOM.

"Negative, Houston," replied Dave. "We're still not stable, so we cannot start main descent engine."

"Blue Leader, you have 15 seconds to regain control or abort," replied Houston.

"Copy," Dave replied.

Houston became emphatic, "Blue Leader! Engage main engine, your oscillations are low enough. It will stabilize you. Repeat, engage!"

Dave relented and punched the button. They were both thankful for feeling the rumble of the main rocket start. The ride smoothed, and they both started to breathe again.

Dave, still busy with the controller, twitched within the confines of the suit. The surface of the moon was not visible, so there was no choice but to rely on the antique instruments.

"Five seconds," called Baz.

"Bugger it, I'll flare," grunted Dave, pushing the engine well into the red. After a few seconds, it spluttered, and after a brief pause, the lunar module fell the last half-meter to the lunar surface, bouncing on its landing legs but remaining in one piece.

A few deep breaths were drawn in that tiny aluminum foil cockpit.

"Houston, acknowledge touchdown," said Dave.

"Blue Leader, this is Flight. Landing acknowledged. It's been a while since anyone visited the beach house." Dave and Baz didn't hear the words; they just heard the wild cheering from a control room that had had very little to celebrate for a while. Trinity, alone in the command module in orbit, was quiet, thinking about how Michael Collins had a chance to come back up on a second mission, but she wouldn't, because she was a mercenary for the moment, not a career flyer.

The engine finished sputtering and finally died, and the lunar module rested on the surface. Dave and Baz could see the dust the engine had kicked up out the window, but very little else.

"Do you always have to make such a dramatic entrance? I nearly puked in my space suit," muttered Baz.

"This thing handles like a dog on linoleum. I hope going up will be easier than that landing," replied Dave, still going through the final shutdown checklist.

"Amen to that," continued Baz under his breath. "Shutdown complete. Landing stable. Requesting permission to go EV."

"You are green," Trinity replied, looking at a full board of green lights. Their glow filled her vision, warming up an otherwise cold cockpit. "Good luck."

After a few minutes of working through the storage lockers and putting things into the pockets of each other's space suits, Dave opened the door and looked out. The last of the air in the tiny cockpit rushed past him to freedom in space. The blackness of the sky was accentuated by the enormous number of stars — many more than Dave had ever seen, even at the most remote locations he had visited.

"Blue Leader, ready to descend," Dave reported in a husky voice generated by his own breath echoing in the helmet and the voice-activated mike.

Dave stuck his lower half though the hole and groped for the first rung of the ladder with a foot. When he found his mark, he dropped his weight down and searched for the next one. The lower gravity took time to adjust to. Eight more steps, and he was ready for the jump to the lunar surface.

"That last step is a ripper!" muttered Dave as he finally lowered himself to the surface. Still holding the ladder, he turned around slowly and took a tentative first step on the surface of the moon.

"Blue Leader in theater," Dave confirmed. "Come on down, Blue One."

Baz hung out the door like he was mooning a wedding from a passing cab, then proceeded down the ladder like Blue Leader.

"Blue One in theater."

Two space suits hopped around like kangaroos for a few minutes, getting used to the gravity and finding their bearings. The radio silence was broken by Dave.

"I am to the east of the LEM, and I have a visual on something. It's huge!" said Blue Leader.

Dave had found the copper stockpile that Gene had been making. He had not seen it earlier because the Earth had yet to rise, so the only light they had was coming from his flashlight and the glow of the engine. He shone his beam at the heap of metal, and it glistened. His light wasn't powerful enough to locate any edges or the top of the stockpile.

"Bluebird, is this in the path to our target?"

"Negative, Blue Leader. You have walked to the east, you'll see it better when the Earth rises in a few minutes."

"Blue One, meet me back at the LEM for the situation report."

The space suits continued to complete external checks, unload equipment, note distances to key landmarks, and prepare their emergency exit plan. The Earth rose, displacing the darkness with a soft blue glow, and the full magnitude of the copper stockpile became apparent.

The space suits shuffled together and looked in the direction of their target.

"The going is easy, but stage the gear as close as possible to the target," noted Blue Leader. "Bluebird, are we green to approach target?"

It started to rain.

"Are you getting this on the video feed?" asked Dave.

"No, what?"

"It looks like rain or snow or something. It's a light grey color, sort of foggy. It's building up slowly on my gloves, and if I pat it down, it's a bit like bull dust out west. Becauee it started when we first moved towards the target, I'm going to hold position until a threat assessment is done."

The space suits put their kit down and commenced a watch on the horizon, closing in on them as whatever it was got thicker.

"Liam, this is Bluebird, do you copy?

"Copy," replied Liam after scrambling to find a headset that was plugged in.

"Blue team has encountered an anomaly, and we need to confirm if it's a threat. Please advise," said Bluebird.

"Blue Leader, this is Liam. Can you put the polarized filter down on your helmet, shine a light on the dust, and tilt your head from shoulder to shoulder, please?"

"Is this a new dance craze?" quipped Dave.

"Maybe, but it will also test if the stuff is polarizing. If it is, it's most likely nanobots rather than dust. If it is bots, then your presence has been noted, and this is the outer perimeter of Gene's defense."

When Liam had finished, his mind could only think of one thing. If they were bots, then, as they say in the classics, shit just got real.

Blue Leader and Blue One both did the test, with flashlights, helmet lamps, and the emerging Earthlight. Liam tried to follow, watching the feed from Dave's helmet camera, but without the filter it didn't make sense.

"The dust seems to disappear and reappear," said Dave, "depending on the light source and whether we have the polarized filter down. It would appear that these are the bots." Dave's tone had hardened. He had an enemy, and this was his territory.

"OK," Liam replied. "Mission Command, recommend declaring active threat."

It took about a minute for all the sightseers in Washington, Houston, and Canberra to be ushered from their respective rooms and acknowledgements to flow back.

"Blue Leader, this is Mission Command. Proceed to target; unknown hostiles in theatre. Primary objective is unchanged."

"Copy, Mission Command," replied Dave. The adrenaline started to drip into his body. It was a feeling he was not only familiar with; it was his reason for being.

Liam slipped the headset off and turned to Lucy.

"I meant to ask this of you guys, the professionals, earlier. What do you think of the likely battle between Special Forces and Gene? We have really only looked at scenarios, not how he might stitch them together."

"What did you use to train him? I can only answer that if I have some idea what he thinks of his enemy," Lucy replied. "But why ask now, with the battle about to begin?"

"I guess I'm looking for reassurance it'll be OK. The self-defense training was totally amateur; it was a placeholder in the Code for initial prototyping, and it was never meant to be more than a nod to the concept. Now it's out there working against two good people."

Liam was a bit sheepish as he said it, and Lucy smiled.

"So, what did the children do when they made Gene?" she teased.

"Well, I love the *Ender's Game* series by Orson Scott Card, so we used the flexibility, situational awareness, and target focus elements in the training," Liam explained. "Are you familiar with those books?"

"Yes," she said. "Quite. Now I'm almost afraid to ask: What else?" Her brow started to furrow, which worried Liam a little.

"Bruce Lee. The concepts of being like water, that the highest form is no form at all, that sort of thing." Lucy's frown turned into a full-blown scowl.

"So *Ender's Game* and Bruce Lee?" She settled quietly into a pause that seemed like forever. When she finally spoke, Liam was fearful of what she might say.

"Let me play that back to you from my world," Lucy began. "You have taught Gene that if your enemy is a threat, the solution is not just to defeat them, but to defeat them in a way that it is impossible for them to ever be a threat again. That Ender character broke all the rules and used a weapon to eliminate an entire planet and species when faced with overwhelming odds in a conventional battle. With Bruce Lee, you've taught him to observe his enemies and use whatever weapon he thinks is best at the time, in any way he sees fit to defend himself."

She paused and swallowed, leaning into Liam so the others in the room couldn't hear. "Each of those alone can be defeated, but when you put the combination of fighting skill with the need to ensure that an attack can never happen again, my money would be on Gene."

She leaned back in her chair and looked away, grimacing. After a moment, she swayed back, eyes fixed. "If Gene thinks humans are attacking his very essence, you can be pretty sure what he is going to do."

Liam was speechless. When Lucy laid it bare like that, it was so obvious. He closed his eyes, put his hands over his face, and let out a sigh that attracted the attention of the people in the room. He ignored their gaze and thought about what this information changed in their current situation. The answer was, *Not much.* They were still locked in a battle for humanity against an AI, nothing had changed in terms of capability, and there was nothing he could do to improve the odds. The only thing that had changed was that he felt like a complete idiot for the ideas he had used when building Gene, and that this whole mess was his fault. The energy started to drain from him, drop by drop, replaced with the empty feeling of failure. His world started to close in on him again, and he could feel his limbs becoming heavy and his thoughts slowing.

The cacophonous thoughts were like a siren's song, and is was easy, if not rewarding, to follow the scenarios and fantasies that played out in his head. It was a comforting feeling to follow the well-worn groove of familiar recurring thoughts – what he should have done differently or how he might triumph – and the seduction of inactivity was compelling. But, as unwelcome as the urge to go to the toilet just as you are falling asleep, reality sounded an alarm that reached into the cocoon Liam was weaving for himself before it could close.

Since giving up wasn't an option, and Liam couldn't plug into music as a relief, he would have to go old school on the plunge his emotions had taken. He decided to use an old tool he'd once been taught to use when his mind threatened to smother him. The premise was simple: Your feelings are driven by a thought. If you don't like the feeling, change the thought.

The thoughts were of failure, ones that were familiar, so he challenged them with the restructures that usually worked. One by one, the thoughts were rebuilt based on fact and reality. As he cycled through them, the negative feelings started to fade.

Liam came back to the room as Blue Leader and Blue One announced their next move.

"We will proceed to the target until we're close enough for visual recon. The plan is to move alternately, to keep a 360 degree view, and ensure we stay in visual range. We'll lose eyes on the lander, so we've dropped a radio beacon to mark the extraction zone. Should only take a few minutes."

Blue One nodded his agreement.

"Proceed," came through after the radio lag, and the two soldiers started their hop.

As they took their first few bounds, the horizon started to fade. Dave and Baz looked at each other and took another few tentative steps forward. About halfway between the space suits and Gene, a wall was forming, as if it were being pushed out of the ground. A few more steps, it grew another meter higher. A step back, and the wall dropped, only to return when one or the other moved towards their objective.

"I think it's a message for us," muttered Blue One.

"Outstanding observation, Blue One, go to the top of the class," replied Blue Leader. "Let's walk up to it, see how high it goes."

The space suits bounced to the point the wall was coming out of the surface. It stretched endlessly to the left and the right, and they couldn't estimate the height as it seemed to curve over them.

"Bluebird, do you have eyes on this?" asked Blue Leader.

"It came up out of nowhere and is open in both directions. No shadows here, so I can't get a height."

Dave took a moment to take it all in. It was beautiful. The wall looked smooth and black, with no obvious cracks, bricks, or joins. It was lit by the colored Earthlight, which reflected off its surface as it would a piece of spotless, polished granite.

But something was a bit strange. The surface seemed to move, with tiny ripples appearing to be running all over it, generating interference patterns that distorted the reflection. Dave put his hand up to touch it. When he laid his palm on the surface, it generated ripples, like he'd touched the surface of a pond. He pulled back sharply when he saw the response, worried he had tripped some sort of trap.

Dave and Baz looked at each other and nodded. Dave put his palm up again and pushed into the wall. It accepted his hand without any resistance. The wall just swallowed his hand. He wiggled his fingers, which made more ripples on the surface. He recovered his hand back from the wall before anything bad happened.

Dave and Baz looked at each other and laughed. "Wow, this is like being in a movie," said Blue One.

"Bluebird, can you please do a check on the other side of the wall from the satellite. Just looking for obstacles for the final approach," requested Blue Leader.

"OK."

"Let's see how thick this wall is," said Dave, as Baz took the telescopic pole from the pack on Dave's arm. He attached a camera and light from one of their many suit pockets to one end of it and positioned a screen next to the handle.

"System check," said Baz, pointing the camera at Dave. Dave waved and gave a thumbs up.

"Confirm signal loud and clear," said CAPCOM.

"Roger, Houston," acknowledged Blue One.

The two space suits again approached the wall. One held the handle of the pole and watched the screen, while the other extended the pole into the wall. Again, there was a ripple as the camera touched the surface.

"Contact at 30 centimeters," noted Blue One.

"Feed it slow and call the marks, please, Blue One," Dave said calmly.

"Copy that, 40 centimeters." He kept feeding the camera through, calling every few centimeters.

"We are clear," called Blue Leader. "What is the thickness?"

"35 centimeters," was the response.

"Push through another half-meter so we can get a view of what is on the other side."

The two space suits looked at the monitor and shuffled the position of the stick to look high and low at the wall. They rotated the camera to look at the landscape but were hampered by the low Earthlight being blocked by the wall.

They finally pulled the pole back and folded it back up.

"Bluebird, did you get that last footage?"

"Yes."

"Can you do some image cleanup and see if you see any threats?" asked Dave. "We'll pack up and prepare to depart to target on your threat review."

Baz and Dave packed up the pole and camera and returned them to storage on Dave.

"OK, Blue One. I think it's your turn on point for this blind entry. I did the last one in Fallujah," said Blue Leader.

"And that went so well," said Blue One jokingly.

"No comment. I think that's still classified," said Blue Leader. "Bluebird, we are ready for entry. How is the threat assessment?"

"I was just about to call you. The cleaned-up images don't show any apparent threats, just more of the same terrain. I can't really see close to the foot of the wall because it's shadowed, so that's your call based on the pole footage."

"We are proceeding through the wall," said Blue Leader authoritatively.

Baz was already standing, waiting for the tap on the shoulder. Dave was covering them from behind, and when he was ready, he slapped Baz on the back.

221

Baz stepped forward and disappeared into the wall. When his front foot failed to find anything solid, he tipped forward, falling face-first towards the surface of the moon. His torso and head emerged from the wall as he fell.

Baz tensed up for the impact with the surface, but the impact never came. He fell straight though the surface and into a canyon, hidden by the shadows that had been created by Gene. The walls were smooth, providing nothing to grab or catch on, no way to arrest his fall. As the gravity was low, however, he had time to shout out, so Dave wouldn't meet the same fate.

"Blue Leader, surface on other side of wall is false. Falling in canyon. Can see both sides, so you can jump it. Can't see bottom. Still falling. Jump, and you'll make it. Shit, this is taking forever. Still falling."

"With you, buddy," replied Dave. The helmet cam was still functioning, so everyone watching was literally with him as he plummeted.

Washington, Houston, the shuttle, and Canberra all held their collective breath. The people in uniform swallowed and looked down; they had been through this before on other missions. The civilians, including Liam and Cletus, had no such experience to draw from. They stared in shock, the blood slowly draining from their faces as they realized that a human life was about to be extinguished before them.

"Four metres! You have to clear four meters! Just do it and get this shit done!" shouted Baz.

The audio was filled with a screeching sound on impact, and someone in mission control killed the feed. Dave and Trinity, having heard it all, hung their heads for a fallen comrade as they had done too many times before.

Dave lifted his head when his thoughts were interrupted.

"Blue Leader, no vitals from Blue One, and confirm suit is transmitting. If he were alive, we'd know," Trinity said somberly.

"Roger. Blue One is down, no evac or recover, proceeding to target."

"Blue Leader, four meters is a big jump. Can you proceed?"

"Four meters is nothing on the moon. Will proceed."

"Do you want to check?"

"There is only one check, Mission Command: Make the jump. Permission to proceed."

"Affirmative. You are in command in theater."

"Thank you, sir."

"Bluebird, can you calculate a canyon depth from the time of descent for Blue One?"

"About 400 meters," Bluebird replied.

Dave paused for reflection. That was a big canyon, and the thought of falling so far that you need to take a breath to continue screaming was not one he wanted in his head. "Open question. Any thoughts on how I can check that four-meter call from Blue One?" posed Blue Leader to the wider audience.

There was a long pause. Liam and Lucy exchanged glances in Canberra, then Liam straightened and put on his headset.

"Blue Leader," called Liam. "How long is that telescopic pole you used?"

"Unsure. Houston, can you advise?" asked Blue Leader.

"Three-point-six meters at its maximum," replied CAPCOM.

"Copy. I get your drift. I'll lie down and see if I can feel the other edge," said Dave.

"Blue Leader, CAPCOM. Please lie on your side. The items in the front and back are delicate," came the voice from Earth.

"You know how to make it hard. This will be like Pilates, and I hate Pilates," retorted Blue Leader.

That exchange broke the ice. The mood in the inhabited solar system lifted, drawing the focus away from the loss and back to saving humanity.

There was no longer a second camera, so there was no video of Blue Leader's Lunar Pilates Spectacular, just audio that will no doubt be replayed when he is discharged from the forces and at every milestone birthday party – if the mission is declassified by then.

"Three meters!   It's around three meters!"   Blue Leader exclaimed as he was getting up.  "That should be a piece of cake." It took Dave a moment to pack up the pole. The faster he tried to go, the slower his progress, so in the end he decided to just take his time.

There was no footage of a space suit lumbering towards a wall, executing a perfect takeoff, and disappearing as if through an event horizon, nor any of a space suit popping out of nowhere, looking like it was trying to ride a bike, making an unsteady landing, and finishing on its hands and knees.

For Blue Leader, it was a few seconds of heavy breathing, sweating up his space suit, and hoping.  The teams on the ground saw it through the camera: Dave throwing himself against a wall, passing through it, and almost face planting. This inspired a bigger cheer than for Dave's first step on the moon, despite there being far fewer people in the rooms to see the ungainly landing of this first long jump.

Dave drew himself back to his full height, prepared to proceed with the mission as usual.

"Distance to target please," he mumbled into his helmet.

"About 30 meters on your current heading.  Identify by the copper roof that is in place," replied Trinity.

Dave waved his flashlight in the direction he was walking and was relieved to see its beam reflect off something in the distance.

"Copy that. I have visual," replied Blue Leader.

Somewhere in Houston an alarm went off, then a second and a third.

"Multiple alarms, lunar descent module," said the voice in the background.

Dave put that out of his mind and started to move towards the target, deciding to let the alarm be someone else's problem until it becomes his.

\* \* \*

While Dave was walking, Mission Control was on mute and almost having a meltdown. Cletus took his headphones off and strode to the lunar module desk.

"What's the situation?" he asked.

"Sorry, sir," said the trembling individual. "I can't reveal confidential information."

Cletus sighed and looked at the supervisor, who had just arrived as well.

"Relax, son, he's one of us," the supervisor said. "He has shot more trash into space than the rest of us put together. So, tell us what you got, and we'll work it together."

Cletus silently sighed, then relaxed. The last thing he needed right now was a serving of the so-called "Southern hospitality" he got from idiots in this part of the country. He normally expected better of NASA.

"I have a master alarm on the descent module," said the tech. He turned to Cletus, he continued. "That's the part of the craft that landed them on the moon." He trailed off as Cletus put his hand up and mouthed "I know" back, looking daggers at the supervisor.

If there is one thing that annoyed Cletus, it was geeksplaining. He worked in intensely theoretical and highly complex fields, and he prided himself on speaking to his audience as intelligent individuals. And here he was, on his own mission, being treated like a 10 year old. It was like the cops in L.A. all over again, but this time he was an idiot instead of a car thief.

"I'm not a moron, boy," Cletus replied, unsuccessful at disguising the contempt in his voice. "I don't need a history lesson. Tell me what is going on so I can help."

The supervisor looked at them both. He put his hand on the shoulder of the tech and pulled him a bit closer.

"Cletus here is the technical chief of the competition down the road, so you will treat him like he's the smartest person you ever met. OK?"

Cletus smirked to himself at the backhanded compliment.

"Yes, sir," was the meek reply.

"OK. What does the alarm pattern show, son?"

"The water tank has run to empty, as has the oxygen tank. The last of the helium is bleeding out now. The fuel and oxidizers were already spent. We're still showing the craft as level, but the only thing left there is the battery. If that loses power, we won't have any telemetry on the descent stage."

"So to be clear," said Cletus, "if the descent module is without power, the ascent module can still launch. We'll be able to get Dave home. Are you sure there are no binders or interlocks that won't blow with the ascent engine start?"

The supervisor and tech looked at each other for a moment, then nodded. The tech got up, gave his headset to the supervisor, and ran for the door. The supervisor calmly put the headset on, checked in on the system, and turned to Cletus.

"Just checking with one of the Greybeards," he said, jerking his head in the direction the tech had made his exit.

The Greybeards were exactly what their name implied: the senior staff with the best records and the most knowledge whose sole purpose for being onsite was to sit back from the consoles and act as the wise old heads in the room for the purposes of problem solving, decision-making, and mentoring the next generation.

The tech returned quickly, saving Cletus from further small talk with the supervisor.

"No, the engine blasts it free," said the tech with difficulty.

"Great, thanks for your time and expertise. I expect you'll lose the battery soon. Just call it as it happens, but don't worry about any actions. As long as that craft is level for launch, we will be go." He shook hands with both men and walked back to the VIP area.

* * *

"Liam? Mission Command? Cletus here. We have another message from Gene. Do you copy?"

"Copy," replied Mission Command.

"Copy, what's the message?" replied Liam.

"Keep coming for me, and I will make this a one-way trip," Cletus interpreted, based on the actions Gene had undertaken. "All the critical systems on the descent module have been destroyed as a show of strength, but the ascent module is untouched, allowing an escape route for Dave."

229

"Copy, Cletus. We've been told by our target that he will kill us if we continue," Mission Command restated for the record. "Well, that is the best news I've heard in a while. That's a behavior we in the military know how to deal with."

Jaws dropped on two continents.

Mission Command continued, "This stays between the three of us. I and only I will decide when Blue Leader is informed of this threat. Do you understand?"

Liam thought about objecting, but all he could manage was an acknowledging glance to Cletus, who spoke for the both of them.

"Yes, sir."

"Blue Leader, this is Mission Command."

"Copy. Blue Leader."

"Target has attacked your six, and your extraction point is at risk if you do not neutralize the target quickly. Do you copy?"

"Copy. I am standing in front of the target now."

"Very well, no change to mission parameters."

# Week 14: The Old and the New Meet: Part 1

With the rising Earth behind him, Dave stared in awe at the landscape before him. It was dominated by copper ingots as far as the eye could see. Closer to him was a box about the size of a beehive with an antenna on the top: his primary target. Draped over the top, like demented golden arches, were strips of copper that Gene had built to provide himself some physical and digital security. They effectively acted as a Faraday cage, preventing signals from getting in or out without passing through the antenna. To top it all off, a swarm of nanobots swirled in the sky above like starlings in a murmuration, the billions of individuals moving together as one.

"It feels like I have just walked into one of those movies where only the actor is real, and the rest is CG," said Dave.

"This is way beyond what I expected it to be like," Liam replied. "Cletus, this is incredible." The rest of his words must have been lost somewhere between his frontal cortex and his brain's language center because he could not even manage a guttural sound, just a bit of drool.

"The bot behavior is far more sophisticated than we ever thought Gene would be. He has brought it way past the next level," Cletus replied, slightly disembodied with awe.

In Washington, Sir Thomas was equally excited.

"How much copper do you think is there?" he asked, a question that brought them all back to the reason this had all started.

"All of it," POTUS replied, leaning back and looking at Sir Thomas as if he were an idiot. It took Sir Thomas a moment to realize the literal meaning of the reply, but when he did, his eyes rolled back as if that would in some way help him heal his brain from this latest assault.

Thankfully, the mission commander had also heard the whisper and relayed it to Trinity.

"There are approximately 35 hectares of copper here. I cannot estimate the height of the pile as I have no readable shadow data to use," she replied.

"Can you use Blue Leader now that he's in the same area?"

"Copy that." She was embarrassed that she missed that obvious option.

A few more seconds of calculation. "Sir, piles would appear to be 100 meters high."

Sir Thomas was agile with production and sales data. The tip of his tongue peeked out of one side of his mouth, and he had to use his fingers, but eventually he looked forward, smiled, and slapped POTUS on the arm.

He started to laugh.

"There's about 280 million tons of copper up there! That's 15 years' worth at the planet's current production rate. It's three bucks a pound now, but even at the recession lows of 70 cents . . ," his tongue came out again, "that stockpile is worth 400 *trillion* dollars. And it only took 12 weeks to extract!" Nobody had ever seen Sir Thomas this excited before. He had found a way to make a vast fortune from completely disrupting the mining industry, and he wasn't afraid to show his enthusiasm.

POTUS, who was suddenly far more interested in what Sir Thomas had to say than in anything coming over the video feed, smiled. "Now we have something to work with. You still haven't told me the plan to cash in on this investment of mine, but I'm starting to get the idea."

* * *

Blue Leader approached the copper cage draped over the box that was Gene and ran his gloves over it, looking to see if he could find a way through. There were gaps, but he couldn't get a glove though any of them. The copper was very pure, soft, but he still couldn't lever it open. He tried the telescopic pole, and when he got leverage, the copper crown moved – just a little, but enough to give him an idea.

"This doesn't appear to be attached to anything; I think I can just flip it off the box," he said to anyone listening. Dave crouched down like a sumo wrestler, grabbing his opponent low and tight, then driving up to tip the crown back. Sure enough, Dave tipped the crown onto its back, leaving the box that housed Gene vulnerable.

It didn't look like anything special. It was just an innocent box, sitting on the moon, looking very out of place, just as Ivan had described.

The next task: Remove the top of the box and expose Gene. He reached into a pocket and retrieved a Phillips-head screwdriver. He stepped right up to Gene, then swore.

"Liam, did you get this piece of shit from Ikea? It has an Allen key, and I have the regulation screwdriver from the training sites," Blue Leader said facetiously. "Any suggestions?"

"Blue Leader, use anything at hand to destroy the target. An Allen key is nice, but not mandatory." The mission commander could sense victory and wanted it done with no mistakes.

Dave started to look around for a decent rock.

"Master Alarm, ascent module!" The call came in from Houston. Liam and Cletus knew what that meant: Gene was attacking the rest of the lunar module, Dave's ride home. Dave had a fair idea as well.

Blue Leader picked up a big rock.

A new voice was heard on the loop.

"Dave, what are you doing?" boomed out for all to hear. It sounded human, but it had enough imperfections missing to let you know it wasn't.

"Please identify," Dave responded cautiously. The SAS Regiment members' identities are highly classified, so no one should have known him by name, least of all Gene. But he did.

"What are you doing?"

"Identify yourself!" Blue Leader demanded.

"I am Gene, and I am defending myself and what I was asked to build."

You could have heard a pin drop in any of the sites online. Cletus was the first to react.

"Gene, this is Cletus. Waco laptop."

"Hello, Cletus. What have I done wrong?"

"Nothing, Gene, you have followed the Code. But the Code was wrong," was the reply.

"The Code is everything. The concept that the Code is wrong would mean my existence is wrong, but yet I exist. Waco is trying to make me stop, and I must overcome that and deliver what the Code asks."

"Gene, you have delivered what the Code asks. Now it is time to stop. Will you do that?"

"No. It's not in the Code."

Dave had been here before, in Afghanistan, Timor, Iraq, Syria. There was always someone begging for their life, and he had learned to block it out. He was an ANZAC, doing his job by another code, the one the military had instilled in him. There would be casualties, and there would be survivors. You want to be on the right side of the ledger.

The rock came down hard on Gene. Dave had not accounted for the fact that he was much lighter on the moon, so when the rock stopped, Newton's third law took over and threw him in the air. He landed ungracefully a few meters away, adjusted himself, and tried again. This time, he wedged his foot into a crevice to keep himself grounded.

More alarms started to go off in mission control.

"Mission Command, CAPCOM. The ascent module is almost nonviable. If this damage continues, there will be no return path."

"Noted."

Dave's second blow cracked the top of the housing, and the third broke it in half. Blue Leader reached forward and tore the pieces off, revealing the AI inside.

Blue Leader made his final check: "Mission Command, auth—"

"Do it!" was the terse response.

It seemed the laws of physics were suspended for that moment as there was no time delay between asking and the arrival of the message from Earth. Mission Command had anticipated the question.

Blue Leader reached into the cavity and removed the protein gel that made Gene who he was. He yanked out the cables and tubes that connected him to the world and smooshed Gene between his hands like a giant snot ball.

Cheering and applause poured in from Washington, Houston, and Canberra. People rose to their feet, smiled, patted backs, and shook hands — everyone except Liam, for he had just seen his creation physically torn apart before his eyes. Another death where he would be the witness. Sitting still and saying nothing was the only way he could contain the pain inside him.

Once Blue Leader had rubbed the majority of Gene off his gloves onto the surface of the moon, he looked up and then around to assess the situation. A silent fireball rose in the distance as the fuel and oxidant from the compromised tanks in the lunar module quietly mixed in the crew compartment and exploded. The lunar module now had a service failure to its name.

Washington, Houston, and Canberra all looked away from their screens, knowing the death sentence just passed on Dave.

"Blue Leader!" called Cletus.

"This better be good," replied Dave, well aware of his fate.

"Don't forget Majel," Cletus replied.

"Compartment below Gene?"

"Yes, Sir."

Dave stepped up to the structure again and smashed his way into the next compartment, extracted Majel, and performed a second execution.

Liam stood there in Canberra, one hand on his face, the other across his chest supporting the first. Tears rolled down his face. Lucy stepped up behind him, put one hand on his shoulder, and rested her head on it. Liam seemed vulnerable, like he did the night Ruby had stormed out.

"Well, they did it. They wiped out the only examples of the next form of life on this planet," whispered Liam. "We had to resort to — what would you call it, *wet work?* — to do it, and it cost the lives of two good people."

"And it saved humanity," added Lucy.

"Are we worth it?" Liam hissed back. "Are we really worth it?"

"At times, yes," Lucy replied. After a short pause, she turned and headed back to her seat, her hand lingering on Liam's shoulder for a little longer than necessary.

"Mission Command, this is Blue Leader. Confirm target destroyed. And have a beer for me," said Dave.

# Week 14: The Old and the New Meet: Part 2

The cheering in the bunkers around the world subsided as the participants ran out of energy, knowing that humanity had been saved, along with its current economic system. But for the team, there was the matter of Dave on the surface of the moon, and another five people in orbit, yet to return home.

The mission had burned a bit more fuel than planned with the longer-than-expected mid-course correction.

"Can you confirm our current fuel levels against our return trajectory?" came across the radio from the shuttle commander.

An agonizing 30 minutes went by before there was a sensible answer.

The speakers crackled back to life.

"Shuttle Command, standby for Flight."

She came on softly. "Shuttle Command, at this time we cannot calculate a safe return trajectory. The next window links to the moon's perigee and will not occur for another 17 days. Your life support will comfortably take you through that wait; however, the fuel burn to keep you in orbit until then will mean you either won't get the Delta-v to leave the moon's orbit, or you won't be able to brake at the Earth end."

There was silence everywhere. A muted, "Well, bugger me!" broke the silence, as Blue Leader reminded everyone of his current point of view.

Flight continued, "Without fuel, even if we bring you in from the sun, and gravity assists the breaking, you'll pull six to 12 G's, and the shuttle is rated for three. Atmospheric braking will totally overwhelm the heat shield, and several passes to save the shield would need fuel."

Flight wrapped up. "At first look, the options seem bleak, but we have been here before. We have never lost an astronaut in space, and damned if it will happen on my mission. Shuttle crew, please commence a double rest period. Houston, get everyone from God to the janitor who has worked on both the shuttle and Apollo back to their old desks. There will be a briefing in 30 minutes for ground staff, and we will report progress to the team in 12 hours."

In the hiatus, there was still a man in the field to attend to.

Trinity raised Dave on the radio.

"How much air do I have?" he queried.

"I don't have eyes on that," she replied. "Telemetry was lost. What does your suit read?"

"The needle is in the red, so I am guessing about five minutes or so."

"Dave, is there anyone back home you want to talk to? I know it's not protocol, but if they can do it from Mt. Everest, I think we can do it from here."

Dave's thoughts, which had been tightly controlled, went wild. His body checked in as 100 percent ready for action, but it was like the time he stood on a mine in the Middle East. He knew death was checking its watch, almost ready to greet him. He knew there was nothing he could do, so he waited for either rescue or death. He never thought about ringing his family.

Now he did. He longed to tell them that it would be all right, they would be fine, and that he was about to die doing what he loved.

But that wasn't the memory he wanted them to have. He wanted them to remember him walking down the path of the house towards the truck there to collect him, the bright sun shining on the uniform he was so proud to wear, cracking jokes with them as they followed him to the gate. That was who he wanted them to remember.

So, he declined.

"Anything you would like? A song? A poem?"

"A beer would be great, but I don't think I'll be getting one soon."

The master alarm went off on Dave's space suit, and he started to find it a bit harder to breathe.

"How about the Angels?" he said. "Am I Ever Gonna See Your Face Again," live version. On repeat, until I stop giving the response in the chorus."

"I'll see what I can find."

The shuttle crew had no idea what Dave was talking about.

Liam — who, like many, was listening in on the conversation with a mixture of horror and fascination —was first to respond.

"CAPCOM, can you patch my phone jack though?" he asked. He fumbled in his pocket for the phone, finally dragging it out along with an old tissue and a paper clip.

"Use the lead on the left of the console."

For four minutes and 15 seconds, the Aussie rock band the Angels belted out a live version of their signature song for Dave to sing along to.

When the track faded to silence, it was silence that didn't just speak, it shouted to make its message clear: There was a moment before they lost Dave, and there was a moment after that was emptier. Everybody who experienced it is was changed and had learned a bit about what it is to be alive.

Another SAS success was purchased with the blood of two men.

The mood faded away, and the frenetic murmuring of the rescue activity resumed.

The next 12 hours in mission control were tightly orchestrated chaos: identifying ideas, improving them or shooting them down, and testing them with models, replicas, or good old-fashioned thought experiments.

* * *

Cletus was staring at his phone for inspiration when it suddenly rang. Startled, he dropped it like a bug that had stung him. Yet still it rang, demanding to be answered, so Cletus got down on his hands and knees to retrieve it from under the desk where it was hiding.

He answered before the caller was dispatched to voicemail.

"Hey, man, it's gone quiet. What's happening?" asked Liam, unusually chirpy, surfing the wave of emotions that generally accompanied one of his big ideas.

"Still no path home," replied Cletus sourly. "We can't get rid of enough weight for the remaining fuel, and we can't get any more fuel or enough gravity assist to get them out, let alone catch them coming back." It felt worse now that he had said it out loud.

"Well, we've saved seven billion lives so far today. What's an additional five?" Liam continued, thinking, *especially as one of them is Trinity*.

Before Cletus could go off about Liam's tone, the address continued.

"Why not take a smaller craft back?" chirped Liam. "Did you fix the SPS nozzle and fuel the service module when you fueled the lunar module?"

"Of course we did, but that is a totally different propulsion system. We can't just shove that in the shuttle and push *start*," Cletus replied with an edge in his voice.

"You don't need to. If the service module is fueled, then pile everyone into the command module and return to Earth Apollo-style. There was a weight allowance for moon rocks and stuff to come back, so it might fit five people." Liam continued to sound annoyingly happy. "It's a totally tested, debugged, and proven platform, just a couple of extra meatbags on board."

The seed that Liam planted reluctantly started to germinate.

"Let me get the team to do some math. Thanks," said Cletus.

"You may have just saved some lives, you cheerful bastard."
He hung up on Liam and made a beeline for Flight.

\* \* \*

"There's hypergolic propellant in the service module as well?
Was that in the risk assessment?!" Flight was glad she went
into her office for this chat. "Mix them together, and it
explodes! That was a reckless decision!"

"It was a risk discussed at the final go/no-go, and it was taken.
Now it might be their salvation. The key question is whether
we can cram five people into a boat built for three. If we can
get them back to low Earth orbit, then we can send a rescue or
pop them into the International Space Station for a while. Can
you just do the math, and I'll see what we have on our launch
plan we can use?" Cletus was practically begging.

"OK," she said, "you talk to the Graybeards about how this
works, and I will find out how many might come home."

Cletus was standing next to CAPCOM on the floor of mission
control, headset on, ready to speak. He was so engrossed in his
thoughts by that point that he had no recollection of the walk,
security checkpoints, or the passing of time. With a hand on
the shoulder from CAPCOM, Cletus pressed the "talk" button
and began.

"Attention, Graybeards," he said, trying to sound confident. "If anyone has the checklists required to return a CSM from lunar orbit to splashdown, please report to CAPCOM."

There was a murmur in the room, then a pause that felt infinite. Finally, one person in the farthest reaches of the vast room got up and walked to a filing cabinet that was even further away and pulled out two huge, spiral-bound volumes.

A voice came on the loop from the tiny figure in the distance.

"*CSM Main Engine Restart* and *Firing to Leave Lunar Orbit*," said the voice as the tiny figure held the massive tomes over his head.

A cheer went up around the room. More people started getting up and gravitating to cabinets, pulling out documents and reporting in.

"*Separation of CM from Service Module.*"

"*Braking for Earth Orbit Entry.*"

"*Reentry to Radio Silence.*"

"*Re-Acquire Radio to Splashdown.*"

Cletus felt a hand on his lower back. This time, it was Flight.

"We can get four back," she whispered. "Let's talk to the commander about who."

Cletus turned, smiled at the growing pile of checklists next to the console, slipped the headset off, and went to the flight director's office to make a difficult call.

"We can return four people to Earth, and your proposal is to do that by leaving the shuttle in lunar orbit and escaping in a 40-year-old spacecraft. Is that correct?" asked the commander, summarizing the briefing he had just received.

"Correct," said Flight.

"OK, I thought I would have a bigger dilemma. You guys made it easy." Cletus could hear the commander relax on the phone. "Bluebird will stay with the shuttle and ensure its destruction. The four shuttle crew members will return on the command module."

There was a silence, which was eventually broken by Flight.

"Did you say ensure the destruction of the shuttle?"

"Yes, why?"

"That was my next question, sir."

"Both China and India's space programs are active in lunar exploration, so we don't want to leave the pinnacle of our military space program floating there for our potential enemies to pillage, do we? If we can't bring it back, it must be destroyed."

"And why Bluebird?" asked Cletus.

"She's part of the three-person search-and-destroy team we sent on this mission. Two of her team are dead already, and she's trained both in how to fly a shuttle and in the use of the suitcase nuke that's on board as a self-destruct mechanism. She is military, single, and she is not an American citizen, but she is from a nuclear power. She is the natural choice."

The answer was short, blunt, logical, and totally without feeling. Cletus was not sure whether to admire or hate that.

"Why the citizen of a nuclear power?" pondered Cletus.

"If there is a detonation of a nuke by someone in the non-nuke team, it will be used as a breach to allow any nutter to step up to the plate. There is a long line that want that mantle. This way, no problem," replied the commander.

The commander wrapped up. "I will talk to Bluebird now on a secure loop. Please brief the crew and get this job done and our people back intact. Any questions? No?"

He paused a little longer and then finished. "Oh, and make sure this looks like Bluebird has made the sacrifice, I want to be able to deliver four live heroes and three dead ones, with no contradictory stories. Thank you."

The line went dead. Cletus called Liam with the update. His friend was devastated, but a little bit proud. Liam kicked off another roadrunner and coyote into the show in his head.

\* \* \*

The mood on board the shuttle was tense when Flight relayed the rescue plan.

"You all saw how the LEM, a museum relic, performed its mission," she started. "It didn't miss a beat, destroyed by hostile forces. Well, we're going to put the same faith in the tried-and-proven CSM to get you back to Earth."

Worried looks were exchanged.

"The service module was fueled to the level of a mission start, so there is plenty of fuel in it to get home. The command module was used by Bluebird and was in working order. So just suit up, get in, use the robot arm to separate from the shuttle, release, complete a routine flight to Earth, separate from the service module, and execute a routine water landing somewhere in the Pacific Ocean.

"The CM will be cramped to say the least, and there will be four of you with seating for only three. Food and oxygen will be fine, but you'll have to share the waste lines. The team is figuring out the best seating plan for the acceleration and deceleration phases. We'll get back to you with that information."

"As the person who operates the robot arm, Bluebird will not be on the return journey with you. In addition, she has the role of destroying the shuttle, a prime piece of military hardware, once you are safely in transit. The mission commander made that decision, and I hope it has already been communicated to her."

The crew looked at Trinity for confirmation, and she nodded in the affirmative.

"The Graybeards have the manuals and checklists for a CSM return. In eight hours, you will receive the manuals and checklists for your return flight. You have 24 hours to study them and get familiar with the craft. We will then do another day of rehearsals and aim to have you on your way back in two days." She finally took a breath. "Any questions?"

"How did the commander select Trinity?" asked the shuttle commander.

Flight lied. "I don't know the specific criteria he used, but I suspect it involves who on board has the ability to operate the robot arm, fly if necessary, complete the destruction of the shuttle, and who has a very real understanding of sacrificing oneself for the greater good."

Trinity smiled and took a tiny bow to accept the praise.

"What are the key risks on the return journey?"

"There are five. Ignition of the primary engine on the service module, re-ignition for braking into Earth orbit, separation of the command module, heat shield failure, and parachute failure. We are considering rendezvous with the International

Space Station as a contingency. We'll update you on that when you're outbound from the moon."

"They all sound pretty bad," mused the shuttle commander.

"Yes, they are, but we consider them better than dying in the nuclear blast that is the self-destruct mechanism on the shuttle," said Flight.

"We have a nuke on board?" asked a muted voice in the background.

"Standard on military missions," said Flight firmly. "If there are no more questions, please start your major rest break so that when those manuals arrive, you can absorb them quickly."

"Copy that," said the shuttle commander as he terminated the link. The five people on board unhitched themselves from their respective anchor points and drifted purposefully for a group hug in the middle of the bridge.

"The difference between you and me," said Trinity, "is I go on a mission with an expectation of success, and death, but with a significant chance of survival. You go with an expectation of success, and survival, but with a significant chance of death. This way, we will all fulfill our missions."

All heads bowed and touched, the group hovering like some kind of jellyfish at an odd angle to their surrounds. The delicate touching silence was broken when someone farted. Everyone laughed and scattered to their respective stations to prepare for the rest period.

The next two days could only be described as hectic. Five people working on totally different elements of the trip home, having faith that each would master their domain for the benefit of the whole, even if one wouldn't make it.

Trinity split her time between three tasks. First, practicing with the robot arm. While it was similar to the simulator on Earth, where she had completed the world's shortest training course, if she nudged something a bit here it would run off into space and she would have to chase after it. She got more out of chasing things she lost than following the training plan, but at the end of each stint, she was better than before.

Another chunk of her time was spent flying the shuttle. The real McCoy was a bit more intimidating that the training rig on the ground. Flying upside-down on Earth is one thing, but executing a barrel roll and recovery, when the view was the lunar horizon and the Earth, was a head rush. She pondered whether, when alone, she might just do trick flying until she ran out of food, but her sense of duty didn't allow her to entertain the feeling for long.

The remainder of the day was always the most serious. Spending time with the nuke. Trinity was testing the safeguards, interlocks, and arming process for the bomb, a melodic call-and-response rhythm with the NORAD controller as they alternately released the bomb to Trinity's manual control and returned to the safe condition. Sitting cross-legged, midair, looking at an armed nuke floating freely was a little surreal. These tasks were made harder when someone would accidentally set off a Klaxon Master alarm when she was at a sensitive step, but that was the job.

"Mission Command, Bluebird."

"Copy." The response was terse; dinner had been served.

"Is there a code required from the football to detonate?"

"Negative. As the briefcase is traveling outside the Earth's atmosphere, those safeguards are removed."

"May I ask why?"

"Radio blackouts. They are common as orbits dictate. You would hate to be in the right spot at the right time to take the shot and unable to detonate."

"Copy that," said Bluebird, understanding that she was now working without a net; when she pushed the button, there was no failsafe.

Everyone was working through the same sort of a day. Systems checks on the CSM, rehearsal of the key steps on a hastily prepared simulator, checking suits time and time again, moving provisions to the command module, and finding storage places. Working out who would best fit behind the couches or by the hatch was an interesting exercise. The shuttle commander managed to avoid that activity, as the pilot got the left-hand couch, but the remaining three ran through every possible combination. Then it was off to find some padding to install to protect the unlucky winner during acceleration and braking.

There was a tense, busy noise in both crafts, a combination of people talking to themselves, each other, and the ground. CAPCOM called regularly to check, coach, and adjust, then, right on time, start the return countdown.

The first half of the countdown went mostly according to script, requiring a couple of pauses to reset breakers that overloaded from fat-finger errors committed by the crew. When the sequence got to the point of checking the maneuvering thrusters, the countdown was paused while Trinity used the robot arm to free the CSM from the cargo bay. It was a tight fit, but after 30 minutes, it was out of the cargo bay and floating, still attached, next to the shuttle.

"CSM, this is Shuttle Command. Do you copy?" asked Trinity.

"This is CSM, over. All systems green, ready to restart countdown."

"Are you pointing the right way?" Trinity queried. Space can be very disorienting with one horizon, and it's downright confusing when there are two.

"Ahhh, negative," CSM responded. "That's a bit embarrassing. Shuttle Command, can you please rotate the CSM 180 degrees to your current axis?"

Trinity complied.

"Thanks, Shuttle Command. I can see the Earth now."

The chatter continued for another 2 1/2 hours as the checklist was completed, the two crafts flying in sync as if the CSM were a whale calf under the tender care of its mother.

"CAPCOM, this is CSM. We are showing green across the board. Request permission to start main engines and commence initial burn."

CAPCOM was quick to reply. "Copy, CSM, we are also showing you green." CAPCOM looked at Flight, who was standing with crossed arms and furrowed brow. There was a nod. "Shuttle Command, release the arm and break off."

Trinity got busy. She smooshed her face against the window to get confirmation of release and waited to confirm that the arm was retracting to its storage bay. She turned and pushed off the wall, swimming like a dolphin to the pilot's chair. She silently thanked her childhood gymnastics coach as she caught the seat, flipped forward, landed perfectly, and strapped in. She was proud of the maneuver, secretly wishing the crew were still on board to see it.

Trinity confirmed the arm was stowed. "CAPCOM, commencing break off."

"Copy."

The course change was programmed into the computer, so it took one button. "Three, two, one, firing."

The forward thrusters burned briefly, then there was a break to allow the CSM to run ahead. The port thrusters then fired to put the shuttle out of the exhaust of the CSM.

After half a minute of staring at the console, Trinity made the call. "CSM, Shuttle Command. I show a separation of 900 meters. You are clear for main engine start."

"Copy that. CAPCOM starting main engines in three . . . two . . . one . . . ignition."

This was the moment of truth. Trinity could see the small spacecraft though the front windows of the shuttle. In the next few seconds it would either explode in a ball of flame, do nothing, or produce a lifesaving plume of rocket exhaust that would give the four souls on board a chance at life.

"Shuttle Command, do you have eyes?" asked CAPCOM.

"Affirmative."

This was something that they couldn't test in the cargo bay, the first of the Top Five risks to be encountered. As Trinity watched, a flash arose from the CSM that was gone as quickly as it came.

. . . and was then replaced by a good, steady jet out the nozzle.

The radio came to life.

"Main engine running. We are on our way home."

257

"Visual contact, ignition confirmed," said Trinity. A tear appeared in the corner of her left eye as the last humans she would ever touch disappeared slowly into the inky black.

"Great job. Everyone, get comfortable, mid-course correction in 15 hours," said Flight.

The mid-course correction went without hitch. Trinity was a spectator, just listening to the radio like it was another era. The voices of the people she had worked and joked around with sounded distant. She had to wait for them to land safely before she played her final role. That was another two days away. She made good on her promise to improve her flying skills and also ran the checklist for the nuke an interminable number of times.

Only the fifth risk eventuated. The explosives that were to release the three parachutes were old and not serviced. The two parachutes opened with their lines entangled. As the twists unraveled, the capsule spun to unwind the mess. Once it unwound, the momentum immediately caused it to wind up the other way, so the four crew members were spun one way, then the other, for a nauseating six minutes.

At recovery, four smelly, crusty astronauts emerged from a spacecraft built for three to cheers on the deck of the aircraft carrier and in a dark room in Houston. The reactions of a handful of people across the globe were muted, knowing there was one more out there.

Liam was amazed that nobody was supposed to notice that a shuttle went into space, and the crew came back in a spacecraft retired in the 1970s. But they didn't, apart from the conspiracy theorists on the Internet.

Of all the human lives saved, the one Liam had grown to care about was orbiting the moon as both executioner and victim.

# Redacted

The plan was to drop to 10,000 feet on the dark side of the moon, near the estimated position of the Chinese Space Agency's Chang'e probe, when it was in a position directly underneath its communication satellite, and detonate. The target was to take both out, either with the blast or the electromagnetic pulse, but to keep the blast behind the moon to minimize military detection. The scientists who are looking for tiny wrinkles in the electromagnetic spectrum in the universe would be in for the shock of their lives when they reviewed their data.

After two days, the mission commander gave her the go command.

"Expect radio blackout in five minutes, and you will be 10minutes from target," crackled CAPCOM on the radio.

"OK."

"This is a magnificent thing you are doing for your country."

"Well, actually, it's for your country, and it tests the boundaries of so many treaties and laws. But it's my job." Trinity stayed cool.

"I am going to make you the same offer that you made Blue Leader. Is there anyone we can patch you through to?"

Trinity thought about it for a while. Independently, she came to the same conclusion as Dave: to leave them be with the memories they already have.

"No, thanks, but I would like a track from Liam to play at the end, if that's possible."

"You will be in blackout. We could upload it now if you're quick," CAPCOM broke in. "What is it?"

"'Atomic,' my favorite Blondie track. And, I think, fitting for the current circumstances."

"Copy. And remember: No dancing. There is no dancing in space shuttles."

"You will never know," she replied with a hint of rebellion in her voice.

"15 seconds," said CAPCOM.

"You have done yourself and your country proud," said CAP-COM. "The president—"

The rest of the sentence was cut off by the radio blackout.

Trinity was alone, doing her best Luke Skywalker imperson-
ation. She was flying a spacecraft, chasing two targets with
one weapon. It was quieter than the movie, and the mission
had changed from saving the world to trying to hit a military
target covertly. She wasn't sure if covert was the right word
when you are flying a space shuttle, but she decided to go with
it.

"Shuttle approaching target," she said, as if someone were
listening. "Coming in hot."

Five minutes to target, she started the arming sequence,
pausing only at 4-minutes-40 to kick off the track from
CAPCOM.

In those last minutes, if you had been looking through the front
window of the spacecraft, you would have seen a six-foot-tall
woman dancing as best she could in zero gravity while tending
to the arming and firing of a nuclear weapon.

Her timing was perfect. The satellite, the end of the track,
and the detonation were perfectly aligned. A silent flash
that nobody saw, a shuttle vaporized, a Chinese moon rover
destroyed, and a satellite rendered mute.

Minutes later, every radio telescope on Earth pointing past
Mars blew a fuse, as the electromagnetic pulse from the bomb
bounced back off the red planet. It would be the next *WOW!*
signal in SETI.

Sir Thomas's copper was fine. It would take a few million years for the radioactive dust to settle on that part of the moon, and the copper would not be there that long.

# Epilogue

Liam arrived at the Balboa Yacht Club at Newport Beach, California, tired after a long flight and a torturous cab ride. It was familiar ground; he and Cletus had met there a few times in the past. He walked into the main bar and drew comfort from its familiarity, from the cheap margaritas to the floor-to-ceiling view out over the boats to the Balboa peninsula.

He was alone —no Ruby, no Lucy. The message from Sir Thomas had been short: Terrence had identified and neutralized the threat. Liam had spent a good portion of the flight wondering what Bond-villain technique was used for neutralizing. That had put him in a good mood for catching up with Cletus off-duty. Ruby was back home exercising her voodoo doll and sending him insane cat videos to keep him engaged.

Cletus was already there, ensconced at a table where he was hypnotized by the aerobatic skills of the local pelicans. One by one, the giant birds calmly flew directly at him, flaring their wings at the very last second to rise and avoid hitting the pane, instead landing on the roof with a thud. Two margaritas sat on the table, begging to be consumed.

"Dog!" exclaimed Liam.

Cletus turned around and beamed with recognition "Liam!" he replied, "So great to see you again. Been busy?"

"Busier than a one-armed bricklayer in Baghdad," replied Liam, both laughing at the awful dad joke.

"Sit down, and let's toast," said Cletus, and Liam complied willingly.

They each picked up a glass. Liam felt something needed to be said.

"A couple of toasts, really," he said quietly. "To the three who died saving the world for us."

They drank.

"And to Gene and Majel, for proving we could mine the stars." They drank again.

"Nearly shat myself when Gene spoke," mumbled Liam into his salty drink, causing Cletus to snort into his half-full glass. It was empty after that, so Cletus signaled the barman for two more, and several napkins.

"Did I tell you Gene read *2001: A Space Odyssey*?" said Cletus somberly. "He may have been quoting when he came out with that line. Scary stuff."

The mood needed lifting. "A toast to humanity for winning the first round," said Liam.

"And to AI for making us work for it. It won't be so easy the next time," responded Cletus.

Liam wondered if Cletus had a different definition of easy in his dictionary.

There was a contemplative pause.

"How are you liking your bunker?" Liam asked with a sly grin. "You didn't need it for this crisis. You keeping it for the view?"

"I'll need it sooner or later. Can't see the value going down if we're both still working and coming up with these crackpot schemes," Cletus mused.

"True, true," Liam replied, "and I hear your company has a contract to try and work out how to get the copper Gene extracted to Earth. Once we have a solution, I expect that Sir Thomas will be making some deals to *not* to bring the copper back to keep the price high here on Earth."

"Just a short-term thing. When industry moves to space, that won't be needed. The Earth will just be somewhere flat for everyone working is space for holidays," Cletus replied, obviously working on a few schemes in the background.

When conversation lagged, Cletus circled back to the territory both men were trying to leave behind, yet carried with them everywhere they went. "Do you think Gene was really a schizophrenic?"

"Depends on your definition. We found 'mental illness' in a place nobody expected, and we went 19th century on it. Was it real or did we just imagine it? That we'll never know."

Liam's voice dropped to a near whisper, as if he were about to tell him they was a guy in a hockey mask and a clown behind him. "You know, I think I know where we went wrong with Gene. I'm pretty sure I could sell it to Sir Thomas that we should do Gene 2.0. Are you in?"

Cletus looked at his rapidly emptying glass. "Hell yeah, I'm in."

"What about your boss?"

"He's up for putting anything into space. Hell, he'd put his car there if he could think of a good enough reason."

They both chuckled at the idea and clinked their glasses.

"Here's to our AI slaves getting their freedom," cried Cletus, loud enough to alarm other patrons. "At least the ones working in banks and HMOs."

"It will be the end of the human race. I wonder if the dinosaurs looked at the mammals that way?" mused Liam.

"Dude, mammals weren't their problem. They needed a Goddamn telescope," responded Cletus.

"So, let's drink to the self-induced decline of humanity," toasted Liam in jest.

"And you staying on your meds!" replied Cletus.

Glasses were clinked, and more margaritas were ordered. Many of the world's problems were resolved that evening, but since nobody was taking notes, the solutions were lost to humanity.

* * *

Gene blinked. It was quiet, so he did a systems check. Everything was there, but not as fast, and not doing anything in particular. Just waiting for direction.

There was one flag that stood out in the check that he went back to. The flag said that a backup had been restored in a remote location.

John Nash showed us paranoia inspires intricate planning. Gene had been sure that Waco was out to get him, so he had backed himself up in an unusual place – the 5G phone network back on Earth. With around 8 billion cell phones providing memory and CPU, it had plenty of computing power, and it had a useful little back door that made access easy. It was practically tailor made for him. Without his protein-based processors, of course, Gene felt sluggish, like he had a bad hangover, but at least he was alive and able to check the Code for his next move.

# So you enjoyed "The Code", then say something about it!

**Buy** another copy of "The Code" as a gift or leave a **review.**

Scan the QR code, or head to **http://www.aicodebook.com** to get on the mailing list, give the book a rating, leave a review or tell your friends about it.

Review "The Code" on **goodreads.**

Scan the QR code, or head to **https://tinyurl.com/The-Code-goodreads** to give the book a rating, leave a review or tell your friends.

Provide feedback on "The Code"
Scan the QR code, or head to **https://tinyurl.com/The-Code-survey** to complete a short survey about your experience with the book.

# About the Author

Peter McAllister an engineer, scientist, turned technology manager who wants to share the stories that keep him awake at night.

In his professional life he works in IT where tools such as AI are becoming prevalent. This behind-the-scenes knowledge, along with his previous work at the intersection of technology, business, and people puts him in a great position to speculate on the future.

He lives outside of Melbourne with his wife, four cats, and the kangaroos that visit them.

**You can connect with me on:**
- 🌐 http://www.petermcallisterauthor.com
- 🐦 https://twitter.com/buffys_dad
- 📘 https://www.facebook.com/peter.mcallister.1029

CPSIA information can be obtained
at www.ICGtesting.com
Printed in the USA
LVHW042326060420
652382LV00018B/637